QUARTZ CREEK RANCH

# THE LONG TRAIL HOME

QUARTZ CREEK RANCH

# THE LONG TRAIL HOME

**Kiersi Burkhart and
Amber J. Keyser**

darbycreek
MINNEAPOLIS

Darby Creek
A division of Lerner Publishing Group, Inc.
241 First Avenue North
Minneapolis, MN 55401 USA

For reading levels and more information, look up this title at www.lernerbooks.com.

Images in this book are used with permission of: © Barbara O'Brien Photography (girl with horse); © iStockphoto.com/Piotr Krześlak (wood background).

Front cover: © Barbara O'Brien Photography.
Back cover: © iStockphoto.com/ImagineGolf

Main body text set in Bembo Std regular 12.5/17.
Typeface provided by Monotype Typography.

**Library of Congress Cataloging-in-Publication Data**

Names: Burkhart, Kiersi, author. | Keyser, Amber, author.
Title: The long trail home / by Kiersi Burkhart and Amber J. Keyser.
Description: Minneapolis : Darby Creek, [2017] | Series: Quartz Creek Ranch |
    Summary: Twelve-year-old Rivka is tired of everything about being Jewish, but
    during a summer at Quartz Creek Ranch, she is inspired to explore and embrace her
    heritage.
Identifiers: LCCN 2016026632 (print) | LCCN 2016054169 (ebook) |
    ISBN 9781467792561 (lb : alk. paper) | ISBN 9781512430905 (pb : alk. paper) |
    ISBN 9781512426984 (eb pdf)
Subjects: | CYAC: Ranch life—Fiction. | Jews—United States—Fiction. | Self-
    acceptance—Fiction. | Interpersonal relations—Fiction.
Classification: LCC PZ7.1.B88 Lon 2017 (print) | LCC PZ7.1.B88 (ebook) | DDC
    [Fic]—dc23

LC record available at https://lccn.loc.gov/2016026632

PJ Library Edition ISBN 9781541510555

Manufactured in the United States of America
1-43966-33980-8/29/2017

For Baby, the best companion a girl could have

—**K.B.**


For Ruth, writing mentor, critique goddess,
and dear friend

—**A.K.**

# CHAPTER ONE

**Y**et another Friday night when Rivka Simon should be having fun.

Her friends were at the movies.

She was at home for family dinner.

"Come on, everyone," her mom called, urging them to stand around the table.

Rivka's dad dimmed the lights. Her brothers stood at their places. Rivka trudged into the dining room after them, last as usual.

Her mom struck a match. Smoke and the smell of sulfur curled through the room. She held the flame to two white candles in the center of the table. The wicks caught and flared, illuminating the faces of Rivka's family. Her mother's voice rose as she began the Hebrew blessing for lighting candles on Shabbat evening, the beginning of the Jewish day of rest.

Her dad joined in, and then her older brother, Noah. Even nine-year-old Eli. Rivka didn't sing. It was a protest. She wanted to be out with her friends.

Her dad lifted the silver wine glass high above the table and began the second prayer. When they were done singing, he took a sip and passed it to her mom, who took a sip too. Eli drank and gave the glass to Noah, who drank and held it out to Rivka. When she didn't reach for it, he said, "What do you have against grape juice?"

She grimaced.

He was trying to be sweet, but that made her even more irritated. Rivka took the glass from him and took the smallest sip possible. Another protest.

Her mother lifted the golden loaf of braided challah bread and held it over the center of the table so that they could each touch it. Rivka didn't want to, but her mom raised an eyebrow.

Rivka reached out with one finger, frowning.

"Would you like to say the blessing over the challah?" her mom asked.

Rivka shook her head.

Her mother held her gaze a moment before turning to Noah.

He was fifteen and his voice had just changed, and when he sang, he sounded almost like their dad. After the prayer, their mother tore off large pieces of the soft, still-warm bread for each of them. Rivka wanted to refuse, but it was hard to turn down challah, and there wouldn't be any more for the next six weeks. She was leaving for Quartz Creek Ranch on Sunday morning. Challah was absolutely the only thing about Shabbat that she was going to miss.

"So," said her mom, handing around a platter of salmon. "Big weekend in the Simon household. How's the packing going?"

Eli practically bounced out of his seat. "I'm ready!" he crowed. "I'm totally ready to go. I can't wait. I want to be the first one there. Do you think I'll get a top bunk?"

Their dad laughed. It was Eli's first year at B'nai B'rith summer camp, and he had been packed for a week. "How about you, Noah?"

Her brother shrugged. "I'll be ready to go."

Their dad grinned. "Exciting summer for you."

Noah was going to be a junior counselor this year. Just like their dad had been. Just like their mom.

"Be careful you don't end up married!" her mom teased Noah.

It was an old joke. A stupid joke. Their parents had met as junior counselors at the very same summer camp and eventually had their wedding there. Whatever. They were constantly telling those dumb old stories.

"Rivka?"

"What?" she said, mouth full of bread.

Her mom pursed her lips. Again. Her mom had looked like a lemon-sucker for weeks now, at least whenever she was dealing with Rivka. "After you have finished chewing," her mom said in a clipped tone, "you can tell me how your packing is coming along. You won't have much time tomorrow because of Natalie's bat mitzvah."

Rivka swallowed. "I'm not going."

The expression on her mother's face hardened.

Her dad cleared his throat. He'd been doing a lot of that lately too. "We discussed this, Rivka. Your friend Natalie has been studying hard. It's her big day."

"Her parents may be your friends, but she's not mine."

Even Eli stopped eating. His eyes darted around the table, zooming in on the source of the trouble.

"Stop looking at me," Rivka snapped.

Eli winced and stared down at his plate.

Her mother's voice dropped dangerously low. "You will leave him out of this."

Rivka shrugged and tore off another piece of challah.

"If you don't go to synagogue tomorrow morning," her dad said, "you can't go to the party in the evening."

She glared at him across the table. "Like I wanted to go anyway." Out of the corner of her eye, she could see Noah shaking his head in the most annoying adult way ever. Her mom was ready to go volcanic. Eli's eyes squinched up like he was going to cry. She couldn't stand to look at any of them for another second.

"It's not that big a deal," she said.

"Rivka—" her mother warned.

Rivka ignored her and pulled off another huge piece of challah.

"This is about your commitment to our synagogue community," said her dad.

Rivka jumped out of her chair so fast it almost fell over. The candle flames guttered and nearly went out. She felt hot, like the air in the room had thickened. It was smothering her. *They all* were smothering her.

"*Your* commitment!" she yelled. "Yours. Not mine!"

She was halfway to her room upstairs when she yelled back down, "I didn't ask to be Jewish!"

\\\\\\\\\\\\\\\\\\\\\\\\\\\\\\\\\\\\\\\\\\\\\\

Rivka slammed the door and threw herself on the bed. Being twelve was the worst. All the other Jewish boys and girls her age were buried in preparation for their bar and bat mitzvahs. Studying Hebrew. Learning to chant from the Torah. Doing community service projects. Rivka had been doing it all too, working hard for her own bat mitzvah in November, when she would turn thirteen.

Then the terrible thing happened at synagogue.

And Rivka dug her heels in.

No bat mitzvah. No more singing at Shabbat dinner. Definitely no Jewish summer camp. Her mom called it *being difficult*. That's what got her sent to Quartz Creek Ranch. Natalie's mom had suggested it, saying maybe the change of scene would do her good.

Rivka pushed herself into a seated position and picked up the glossy brochure. The cover photo showed a green field full of horses. Inside were various shots of kids her age: collecting eggs from underneath fluffy white chickens, riding ponies, and toasting marshmallows around a fire. It looked a whole lot like Jewish summer camp.

But the description? That was a doozy. It described the Colorado ranch as a camp for kids "struggling to navigate life's challenges." Rivka wanted to gag. "Forging connections through riding therapy horses" was not her idea of fun.

At least there wouldn't be any more family dinners.

And the chickens looked kind of cute.

Rivka surveyed her packing progress. A stack of clean jeans and T-shirts. A couple of flannels. Socks and undies. Pajamas. Brown cowboy boots. Her raincoat with the zip-in fleece liner. A Red Sox baseball hat.

There was a knock at the door.

"What?"

"Rivka—" It was her mom. "Can I come in?"

"I'm changing," Rivka lied.

"Are you okay?" her mom asked through the door. She didn't sound sour or pinched. She seemed almost sorry.

It made Rivka feel like her skin was on too tight. "I'm fine, Mom. Just packing."

After a long silence, her mom asked, "How's it coming along?"

"Fine."

Another silence.

"Really," said Rivka. "I'm fine."

On the other side of the closed door, her mom shifted but didn't leave. Finally she said, "I'll be in the living room if you need me, okay?"

"I've got it under control, Mom," said Rivka.

And she did.

She was positive of it.

All Rivka had to do was get the heck away from her family and their expectations.

They left her alone that night, and the next morning Rivka stayed in bed feigning sleep until the rest of her family had left for Natalie's bat mitzvah at the synagogue. Twenty-four more hours and she'd be on her way out of town.

The clock couldn't tick fast enough.

# CHAPTER TWO

The plane trip was weird.

Rivka had never flown alone before. Usually, she and her brothers sat together and fought over a limited supply of Hi-Chews. But on the long flight from Boston to Denver, she was jammed between strangers. On one side of her was a businesswoman in a pantsuit who bent over her laptop the entire time. On the other was a gray-haired man who fell asleep and snored for the duration.

Flying alone turned out to be super boring. Her mom had been adamant about the no-technology rule at Quartz Creek Ranch. Rivka's phone, which she ordinarily used to text with her favorite cousins, was in her desk drawer at home, and the airline didn't even show a movie on the flight. When they landed, the flight attendant made a completely mortifying announcement that "an unaccompanied minor" needed to get off the plane first.

At the gate, a college-age girl with sunglasses on her head and dark hair in a bouncy ponytail was holding a sign that said WELCOME, RIVKA SIMON in rainbow bubble letters. This was even more embarrassing than the announcement on the plane. That huge sign with her old-fashioned name in those dorky bubble letters made her wish she had thought to sign up for camp with a different one— Clara or Tina or June—anything that would sound less Jewish. Rivka had been named after her great-grandmother. It hadn't bothered her until the incident at the synagogue, but now she winced when her flight attendant–bodyguard said, "Come on, Rivka. Let's get you on your way."

Rivka followed her to the girl with the sign, wondering if she could make up some kind of nickname. She hoisted her backpack more firmly over one shoulder and waited while the airline representative checked the girl's identification and had her sign for Rivka like she was a UPS package.

When that was done, the girl turned to her and

smiled. She wore blue jeans with the legs tucked into well-worn cowboy boots and a bright blue T-shirt that said *Keep Calm and Swim On* in white letters. Quick as anything, she tucked her arm into Rivka's and led her down the concourse. "Hi," she said. "I'm Madison, one of the trainers at Quartz Creek Ranch. So stoked that you're finally here. Fletch has got everyone else in baggage claim. Let's get your stuff and blow this Popsicle stand."

Rivka scrambled to keep up with Madison, who walked as fast as she talked.

"Are you hungry?" the trainer asked.

Rivka's stomach growled, and she nodded.

"Me too. Ma Etty packed us lunch. It's in the van. In fact, she practically packed an entire grocery store so we don't starve between Denver and the ranch. Ma Etty says, *You should always be prepared.*"

"Who's Ma Etty?" Rivka asked as they took the escalator down.

Madison grinned at her. "Only the best horse-woman in all of Colorado!"

Rivka gave her a questioning look. That hadn't exactly cleared things up.

Madison laughed. "Ma Etty is what we call Mrs. Bridle. She runs the ranch with Mr. Bridle, which," she added with a grin, "is what we always call him."

She tugged Rivka toward a group of kids gathered around a pile of duffel bags. A guy around Madison's age stood with them. Probably another member of the ranch staff, Rivka figured. He was tall and muscular with dark skin and wore a cowboy hat pushed back on his head. Rivka could immediately imagine him in an old Western movie, chasing down cows or something.

"I've got her!" Madison announced, and everyone looked at Rivka.

She gave the group a little wave. "Hey."

The cowboy held out his hand to Rivka. It was warm and calloused. He had sad eyes but a kind smile. "I'm Fletch, your other trainer. Pleased to meet you." She suppressed the urge to say *Howdy, pardner* and shook his hand instead, nodding her hellos.

"Well," said Madison, jutting her hip to one side and surveying them. "This is the whole crew. Fletch and I are glad to have you. We're gonna have some fun this summer. Let's do quick intros, and then we'll get your bag and skadoodle. You first." Rivka thought this was her chance for a nickname, but before she could think of anything good, Madison said, "What's your fave thing to do, Rivka?"

"Ride my bike, I guess."

"Mountain or road?"

"I'm from Boston."

Madison chuckled. "Road-biking it is." She pointed to a whip-thin Asian girl with a black braid down her back. "Name and favorite activity. Lickety-split!"

The girl shoved her hands in the pockets of her hoodie. "I'm Lauren and I like roller-skating."

"Cool," said Madison. "Ever consider roller derby?"

"My mom would never let me do that."

Madison gave her a sympathetic look before nudging a pasty, overweight boy, fiddling with a Rubik's Cube in one hand. "You're up."

His eyes stayed glued to the cube. "Sam. Puzzles."

"I've known him for half an hour and turns out he's a genius at that thing," said Madison.

She looked around at the small group. Rivka followed her gaze—Lauren, Sam, Fletch. That was it, but Madison and Fletch suddenly looked panicked.

"Where is she?" asked Fletch.

"I don't know. She was right here a minute ago." Madison turned to Lauren. "Did Cat go to the bathroom or something?"

The girl shrugged and went back to fidgeting with the drawstring on her hoodie.

"Sam?" Madison asked. "Did you see her?"

He shook his head and shrugged too.

To Madison, Fletch said, "Stay here and get Rivka's bag. I'll take a walk around the arrival area."

He strode off, cutting through the crowd of people from Rivka's flight waiting for luggage. Madison turned to Lauren and Sam. "You two stay right here. Seriously, don't move, okay? Keep an eye out for Cat." To Rivka she said, "Let's grab your stuff."

While the two of them waited by the conveyor belt, Madison kept shifting her weight back and forth, scanning the crowd, checking Sam and Lauren, unable to settle. She was so twitchy that it was making Rivka nervous.

"You can go look for her," Rivka said. "I'm fine."

Madison's mouth twisted to one side, considering. "Are you sure?"

Rivka waved her off. "It's cool. I'll get my bag and then go wait with the others."

"Thanks. I can't believe she wandered off like this."

Madison speed-walked the baggage claim area.

The conveyor in front of Rivka rumbled into motion. Five minutes later, she had her duffel bag and rejoined the other kids.

"No sign of the missing feline?" she asked.

Lauren's eyes flicked in her direction, then back to a careful examination of the patterned carpet.

"You're funny," said Sam in a completely flat tone, not looking up from the Rubik's Cube.

"Okay then," Rivka muttered under her breath.

"I meant about the cat joke," Sam clarified.

"I got it."

"Okay then," Sam repeated, still twisting the cube. The yellow side was done. The other sides were multicolored disasters. Rivka peered at him, trying to figure out if he was making fun of her, but before she could say anything else, Madison returned looking flustered, followed by Fletch and someone who could only be Cat.

The girl was wearing cut-off shorts and a tank top. Rivka knew her parents would flip out if she ever wore shorts like that. The corners of Cat's mouth were neon orange from the Cheetos she was popping one after another. Her sandy brown hair was in a messy bun on the top of her head. She looked like a girl who knew how to get into trouble.

"Let's go," said Fletch, shadowing Cat all the way out to the parking lot.

\\\\\\\\\\\\\\\\\\\\\\\\\\\\\\\\\\\\\\\\\\\\\

As soon as they reached the old Econoline van, Cat claimed the entire backseat and put in earbuds. *So much for the no-technology rule*, thought Rivka as she took a spot by the window and curled her feet up on the seat. From Denver it was nearly a three-hour drive to the ranch. Sam solved the Rubik's Cube and got Lauren to scramble it for him again. Madison failed every time she tried to get them into conversation, and eventually she stopped turning around to chat from her spot next to Fletch, who was driving, and blasted country music on the van's tinny speakers instead.

Finally the van rumbled onto a dirt road. Rivka bounced and jostled as Fletch drove between fields that were technicolor green. Off to the left side of the van, the fields turned into forested hills, which turned into mountains unlike anything Rivka had ever seen. The jagged peaks looked almost purple, utterly wild and impenetrable. Patches of snow gleamed in the sun even though it was the middle of June. The mountains looked like something out of a movie.

So did the ranch.

Rivka had assumed the brochure picture was a Photoshopped version of the real Quartz Creek Ranch. Instead, when Fletch parked in front of a big ranch house, she realized it was a cheap paper imitation.

A burbling creek rushed by. The fields were dotted with wildflowers. And the horses . . .

"Wow," she said, as she climbed out of the van and stretched.

Madison grinned at her. "I know. It gets me every time."

Sleek animals grazed in the nearby pasture. Black ones and white ones, gray ones and brown ones. A white and black polka-dot horse kicked up its heels and spun around in a full circle.

"That's Snow White," said Madison, puffing out her chest. "She's my girl."

Fletch opened the back doors of the van, and everyone found their bags and followed the trainers toward two small bunkhouses that stood side by side across the lawn from the ranch house.

"Girls with me," said Madison, waving them to

the cabin on the left.

"Come on, Sam," said Fletch. "We've got the place to ourselves."

Rivka clomped up the steps and across the little wooden porch. The main room of the bunkhouse had a table and chairs, two sets of bunk beds, and a single bed in the corner.

Rivka put her bag on the single bed and looked over at Lauren, who was standing in the middle of the room looking shell-shocked.

"You cool if I take this one?" Rivka asked.

Lauren nodded and put her things on one of the bottom bunks.

Madison waved toward the doors in the back of the room. "We share the bathroom. My room's the other one. Get comfy, ladies, and start thinking of a cabin name."

"We're naming a house?" said Cat, claiming a top bunk. "That's dumb."

Madison shrugged. "You're not the first one to say so, but it's a tradition here at QCR, and it's your first job as a team."

Cat squinted at her. "I work alone."

"You make it sound like you're a spy or something."

The girl put her hands on her hips. "I'm serious. Check the file. State of Ohio. I'm sure it says something like *doesn't play well with others.*"

Rivka expected Madison to get mad about the back talk like her mom would have, but Madison chuckled. "I don't need to know what brought you to the ranch, Cat. My job is to teach you to ride." Cat seemed about to give her more lip. "But," said Madison, interrupting her, "you still need a cabin name."

"How about the Antisocials?" Cat sneered.

Madison grinned at her. "If you can get Rivka and Lauren on board, I'm down for it."

"Well?" Cat demanded, wheeling on Rivka and Lauren.

Lauren took two steps backward and crumpled into the bottom bunk. Rivka stared at Cat.

"How about the Antisocials?" Cat repeated.

Rivka couldn't help but wonder why Cat was at Quartz Creek Ranch. She suspected it was a bit more dramatic than refusing to go through with a bat mitzvah. Cat pulled out another bag of Cheetos and tore it open.

"Sure," Rivka said. "Whatever. The Antisocials works for me."

"Wonderful," said Madison, with a trace of sarcasm. "We have a cabin name."

Cat dumped the contents of her duffel bag on the empty bottom bunk in a jumble. Lauren shrank even farther into her bunk.

"Is there a cabin sign or something?" Rivka asked. Madison tilted her head to one side like Rivka's mom did when assessing what she called the sass factor. "Just wondering," Rivka added. "If there's a sign, no bubble letters, okay?"

Madison pursed her lips. "Are you cool with rainbows?"

Rivka shook her head.

"Got it," said Madison, frowning. "No bubbles. No rainbows. So here's the deal, gals," she continued, glancing at her watch. "We've got half an hour before camp meeting in the main house. Feel free to hang out here and get settled." She gave Cat a pointed look and indicated the shelves and drawers available for storing their things. "I'm heading to the barn because the vet is here checking on one of our pregnant horses." She swiped her sunglasses off the table by the door. "You're welcome to join."

Cat shoved a handful of Cheetos in her mouth. "Gah," she said. "I hate babies."

"You hate baby horses?" said Lauren.

Cat made a show of leaning forward and staring her down. "It speaks."

Lauren immediately went back to unloading her things.

Out of the corner of her eye, Rivka saw Lauren swiping at her eyes with one sleeve and felt a momentary pang for her friends at B'nai B'rith camp. She'd bunked with the same girls for the last three years. They had their inside jokes and secret codes. Now they were getting a new bunkmate, and she was stuck with these two—a crybaby and a crab.

## CHAPTER THREE

**W**hile Rivka and Lauren finished unpacking, Cat flopped onto her pile of clothes, pulled out her smartphone, and plugged in earbuds.

Rivka eyed the phone.

Cat caught her watching. "What?" she demanded, spraying Cheeto crumbs everywhere.

"I didn't think we could have phones and stuff."

"Since when is my phone any of your business?"

Rivka shook her head. "Whatever. Get yourself in trouble. See if I care."

Cat rolled her eyes and went back to her music.

*Antisocial*, Rivka remembered, and she headed out of the bunkhouse.

Lauren followed her outside. "She's intense."

"Yeah," said Rivka, squinting against the bright afternoon sun. A couple of fluffy yellow chickens wandered by, pecking in the grass and making warbling, clucky chicken sounds. Lauren gave them a wide berth.

That was exactly what Rivka planned to do with Cat.

"Do you think she gets into fights?" Lauren asked.

Rivka gave her a perplexed look. "Why would she do that?"

Lauren flushed and fiddled with her braid. "I don't know . . ."

Rivka pushed her curly hair out of her face. "Just leave her alone. You'll be fine."

They crossed the bridge over the creek and headed toward the barn. There was a round, fenced pen on one side and a large outdoor arena on the other. Rivka had never ridden before. Once on a summer vacation in Vermont, she'd begged her dad to let her go on a trail ride for a day, but he'd said it was too expensive.

She heard voices on the opposite side of the barn and headed toward them.

An enormously fat horse was standing in what looked like a very small outdoor stall. The horse was the color of ripe wheat with a pale yellow mane and tail. There was a low metal gate at its chest and rear, and metal bars on either side almost touched its flanks. An older woman with gray hair even curlier than Rivka's stood at the horse's head, stroking its neck and whispering to it.

Madison and several others were clustered nearby. As Rivka and Lauren approached, Madison caught sight of them and waved them over. "You're just in time for the good part!" she said.

A tall, blond woman in a tank top and jeans stood up from where she was crouching by the horse's belly and walked over to a white work truck that said *Carla Randall, Large Animal Veterinarian* on the side in big, black letters. When she opened the locked boxes on the bed of the truck, Rivka was amazed to see what looked like an entire medical clinic inside.

The older woman talking to the horse met the girls with a huge smile and widespread arms. "You're finally here!"

Rivka couldn't help grinning back. She immediately loved the crinkly smile lines around the woman's eyes and mouth.

Madison took charge of introductions. "Ma Etty,

this is Rivka and this is Lauren—two thirds of the newly-named Antisocials."

Ma Etty cracked up, slapping her hands on her thighs and snorting. "Best cabin name in a while," she said through her laughter. Everything about Ma Etty was bouncy. The horse snorted too and tossed its mane in the air. Rivka and Lauren exchanged a look and shrugged.

Madison scratched the horse between its ears. "There, there, Chickpea, it's all good. I doubt they're really antisocial."

"Um," said Lauren, "is that horse named after a bean?"

"Yup!" said Madison. "Ma Etty must be hungry every time she names the animals. Don't even ask about the chickens."

"What about the chickens?" asked Rivka.

Madison faked her exasperation. "I told you not to ask about the chickens."

Ma Etty chimed in. "I name all the chickens for food. And you're right, Madison, I am hungry all the time."

A tall man with salt-and-pepper hair and a deeply lined, bronzed face approached. "You're telling me," he said, holding up his right hand. Lauren gasped, and Rivka could see that his ring finger was missing down to the second joint.

Ma Etty hip-checked the man as he chuckled. "Willard, you stop that right now! Girls, don't you listen to a thing he says."

"Howdy then," the man said, extending his hand. His finger wasn't missing at all. It was a joke Eli would have loved. "I'm Mr. Bridle. We're happy to have you here this summer. I promise I won't let Ma Etty gnaw on your fingers."

Rivka had never seen such goofy old people. Even her parents were way more serious than these two.

"Hey, team," called the veterinarian. "Paul and I are ready over here. Let's see what's going on with this foal."

Madison introduced Rivka and Lauren to Carla, the vet, and Paul, the sandy-haired ranch manager with an epic mustache, and they all gathered around to watch as Carla pulled on a long plastic glove that went all the way to her shoulder. She got Madison to stand close to the mare, holding something that looked like a burly white laptop with a black-and-white screen.

"Before we do the ultrasound, I want to check

her manually," said Carla, lifting the horse's tail with her ungloved hand.

Rivka took a step backward. She might be anti-social, but her parents were anti-pet, and this was looking like it might be a little too up-close and personal for her experience. Lauren's eyes were huge, and for once, she didn't look like she was about to cry. The rest of them looked as casual as if they were all waiting in line to buy popcorn at the movies.

Carla slid her gloved hand under the horse's tail and . . .

"What the what?" The screechy voice surprised everyone, including the horse, who pranced in its tiny enclosure, forcing Carla to step back.

It was Cat, coming around the corner of the barn with Fletch and Sam on her heels. "Did you seriously just put your hand in that horse's, you know—?"

Sam, still messing with the Rubik's Cube in his hand, snorted.

Rivka snuck a glance at the Bridles to see how they would react. Neither seemed fazed. Ma Etty went back to calming the horse. Mr. Bridle strode toward the newcomers. "You must be Catherine and Samuel," he rumbled.

The two kids corrected him simultaneously.

"Cat."

"Sam."

Mr. Bridle scratched the side of his nose. "Well then, Cat and Sam, welcome to Quartz Creek Ranch." He tipped his cowboy hat to both of them. "Today's your lucky day."

Cat cocked her head and swept her hair out of her face. "How so?"

His face lit up. "Come here." He urged both kids to join the group crowded around Carla. Fletch took Ma Etty's place at Chickpea's nose. Rivka could hear him humming to the horse, a tune that reminded her of a lullaby her mother used to sing, and she felt a pang of regret. She had not said a very nice good-bye to her family.

Carla went back to work. Her face twisted in concentration as she felt inside the horse. It made Rivka wince to see how far the vet's arm went inside the animal, but with Fletch singing, the horse didn't seem to mind at all.

The ranch manager caught Rivka's expression and patted her on the shoulder. When he smiled, his mustache twitched like a furry little animal. "Don't worry. Doesn't hurt the horse at all. Carla's amazing." It seemed to Rivka that he turned a little pink in the cheeks when he said this, but maybe it was the hot afternoon sun.

"This foal is in exactly the right position," said Carla, stepping back from the horse and peeling off her glove. She stroked Chickpea's rump. "Such a good mama."

"Gross," said Cat, her face pinching up.

Madison quirked up one eyebrow. "What's not to love about horse babies?" Madison asked, and the girl just shrugged.

"Hey, Carla," said Paul, "are you ready for the ultrasound?"

The vet grinned at him. "Definitely."

He unhooked a probe that was attached to the laptop thingy Madison was holding and handed it to her. "Here you go."

"Turn the ultrasound machine on, will you?" Carla asked, and Paul bent over the controls until a grainy black-and-white blizzard appeared on the screen. She leaned across him to adjust a few of the knobs and dials before squatting next to the horse. The kids clustered around the display.

Carla slid the probe across Chickpea's huge belly.

The image on the screen morphed like a black-and-white lava lamp. Blobs grew and shrank as Carla examined different parts of the foal. At several points, she had Paul take a screen shot and label different things: aorta diameter, eye socket, amniotic fluid.

"I can't even tell that's a horse," said Sam.

"I know, right?" Cat piped in.

"She's close to delivery," Carla explained. "The foal is too big for me to see more than bits and pieces of it."

"Is it a girl or a boy?" Rivka asked.

"You mean a filly or a colt," Madison corrected.

"Uh, I guess so," said Rivka.

Ma Etty, who was standing behind her, must have sensed her discomfort because she put her hands on Rivka's shoulders. "No worries. We should hand out a ranch dictionary or something. Half the time it must seem like we're speaking a different language."

"Horse talk is its own thing," agreed Paul.

"Baby horses are called foals," Ma Etty explained, even though Rivka already knew that. "Females are called fillies, and males are colts."

"We'll have you speaking fluent horse by the time you leave," Paul said with a chuckle.

Rivka liked him already.

"Back to your question," said Carla, standing and curling the cord of the probe around her hand. "I tried to determine the sex of the foal earlier in the pregnancy, but it kept moving around. This one will be Ma Etty's surprise."

"What's your verdict on my surprise?" Ma Etty asked.

"I think we're spot on with timing," said Carla. "It's measuring right in line with our estimate that we're about 330 days into this pregnancy. We're getting close."

Cat let out a low whistle. "That's a long time to be pregnant."

"Yup," said Carla. "Longest horse gestation on record was 445 days."

"Are you serious?" Paul burst out.

Carla laughed. "You know I never joke about horses, Paul, but that was way out of normal. Typical range is 320 to 370 days."

Rivka leaned into the last image on the screen. "This doesn't look anything like a horse."

"I know," said Carla. "After just a few months, the fetus is too big to capture in a single image, but check this out . . ." She hit some keys on the ultrasound machine, and the grainy blobs disappeared. "This picture is from the ultrasound I did early in the pregnancy."

A still image appeared.

A pointy nose. Four little legs, all folded up like spindly origami. A pudgy, round belly.

Rivka could hardly believe the cuteness of it.

Lauren squealed, "It's so adorable!"

Even Cat's face softened.

"You don't hate that baby, do you?" Rivka asked.

A tiny smile swept across the girl's face, making her seem almost approachable.

"No," she said. "Who could hate a squishy little thing like that?"

# CHAPTER FOUR

**A**fter Carla had packed up her things, and Ma Etty had shown Rivka and the others how to give Chickpea pumpkin-flavored horse treats on the palms of their hands, there was still some time before dinner.

"Usually, helping cook is one of the assigned chores here," Ma Etty explained, "but we'll get started with all that tomorrow. Feel free to wander a bit. See you at the big house at five."

Rivka turned to the others. "Wanna go for a walk?"

Cat pointed to a hammock hanging in some trees. "I'm gonna be antisocial."

As she watched Cat swagger off, Rivka was sure that joke would be very old by the end of the summer.

"What about you guys?" she said to the others.

Lauren shook her head, mumbled what Rivka took to be "No, thanks," and made a beeline for the bunkhouse.

Sam didn't even bother to respond. He just glanced at her, shrugged, and then twisted the game cube and brought the green side in order. He weaved across the lawn toward the boys' bunkhouse without looking up.

*I hope he runs into a tree*, Rivka thought, turning to walk along the creek. When she heard him yelp a moment later, Rivka turned to see Sam looking accusingly at a nearby branch.

"Called it," she said to a little brown pony that had wandered up next to the fence.

The pony looked at her and then nudged the fence with his nose.

"What do you want?" she asked, reaching over to scratch under his mane. The pony pushed his nose under the fence, his rubbery lips wiggling their way toward a clump of grass on the other side.

Rivka leaned over and pulled a handful for him. As soon as the pony finished scarfing it out of her hand, he nudged the fence for more. Rivka stood a long while, feeding him grass and zoning out.

She could imagine her brothers at B'nai B'rith camp, singing songs and roasting marshmallows, a first-night-of-camp tradition, but she couldn't think what her parents would be doing.

Funny that she'd never considered it before.

Her parents had six weeks off parent duty. No more forcing her to study every single day for her bat mitzvah. No more homework help. No more meal after meal for her brothers, who never seemed to stop eating. She wondered if they were flopped on the couch in sweatpants, eating popcorn and watching R-rated movies.

The pony waggled his ears and nudged her hand.

"I know. I know," she said. "More grass. Kind of demanding, aren't you?"

\\\\\\\\\\\\\\\\\\\\\\\\\\\\\\\\\\\\\\\\\\

The dinner table in the big ranch house was piled high—baskets of rolls, a green salad, a fruit salad, and a big bowl of vegetarian spaghetti. Mr. Bridle sat at one end of the long table, occasionally reaching up to his forehead like he forgot his cowboy hat was hanging by the door. Fletch was next to him, and they were deep in conversation.

Rivka caught snippets of their talk . . . "cattle prices" . . . "next rodeo" . . . "the mustang threw a shoe" . . . Nobody in her house said things like that. She thought of Paul and his horse talk and decided that was way more fun than learning Hebrew.

Ma Etty bustled around, getting Sam and Lauren to wash up and find their places. Paul came in and started bustling right back. "Come on, Ma Etty. Sit yourself on down. I'll get the milk."

The old woman settled into the chair opposite Mr. Bridle with a sigh. "You're a love, Paul. My feet are killing me."

He grinned at her and also at Rivka when he caught her watching everyone so intently. "Are you going to sit at the rodeo end of the table?" he asked with a wink and a nod toward Fletch and Mr. Bridle. "Or at the *what are we going to name the baby horse* end of the table?"

Rivka hurried to snatch the chair next to Ma Etty.

Paul nodded his approval. "Good call. I knew you were a smart one."

Lauren sat on Rivka's other side with Sam next to her.

"Where are Madison and Cat?" Ma Etty asked, taking in the empty seats.

Lauren shifted in her seat. "They were . . . uh . . . in the cabin . . . um . . . having an issue."

"What kind of an issue?" asked Ma Etty, but just then the front door banged open, and Cat stomped in with Madison on her heels. All conversation around the table stopped.

"Please wash," Madison said to Cat through gritted teeth. She pointed to the sink.

Cat rolled her eyes and flounced to the faucet.

Ma Etty raised one eyebrow.

Madison handed her the smartphone.

"Ah," said Ma Etty, taking the small device.

Cat came to the table, glaring at anyone who met her eye.

"I'll keep this safe for you until the end of the summer," said Ma Etty. "I'm sorry if no one told you about our no-technology policy."

Cat bit into a roll and answered with her mouth full. "I don't see how me being able to listen to my music is any different from him having that stupid cube in his hand all the time." She jerked a thumb at Sam, who was messing with the cube under the table. "I thought you wanted to keep us out of trouble."

Rivka was sure that Ma Etty would tell her to stop being sassy. Instead, the old woman turned to

Sam. "How about we take a break from that during dinner?"

He looked up to see everyone staring at him and flushed pink. "What's going on?"

Mr. Bridle took the cube from Sam but spoke to Cat. "We want you to check in here at the ranch, not check out."

Cat rolled her eyes. Again. Rivka was pretty sure that would get old too.

"Tell you what," said Ma Etty. "Let's start eating, and then Mr. Bridle and I can fill you in on how things work around here. With all the excitement about Carla's visit, we didn't get to do a proper welcome for everyone."

They filled their plates, and for a few minutes, the only sound was the clink of silverware. Rivka could get used to this kind of meal. No know-it-all big brothers. No talking-all-the-time little brothers. *Yes, please!*

After a while, Mr. Bridle cleared his throat. "A toast," he said, raising his glass of milk and waiting until the rest had done the same. "To Sam, Cat, Lauren, and Rivka! A great summer lies ahead!"

"Cheers!" said Ma Etty and Paul with gusto.

Madison gave a little whoop.

No one, Rivka noticed, yelled *L'chaim*.

When they'd toasted and drunk, Ma Etty said, "Ranch life is pretty simple. Ride in the morning. Chores after lunch. Free time after that. We don't have many rules. Be kind. Be careful. Respect everyone and everything."

"And that," Mr. Bridle said, "is pretty much the key to a happy life."

"And horses," Ma Etty added. "Don't forget horses."

Mr. Bridle raised his milk again. "To horses—the key to happiness!"

# CHAPTER FIVE

After dinner, Paul and Madison offered to do cleanup. Sam and Mr. Bridle decided to play chess. Ma Etty and Fletch nabbed separate ends of the sofa and started to read. Cat slipped out of the house to who knows where. Rivka went out to sit on the porch swing, and Lauren followed her.

"Are you excited to ride tomorrow?" Rivka asked her.

Lauren kind of twitched in response. "I guess so."

"Me too."

Rivka kicked one foot to keep them swinging. There was a low squeal from the chain every time they swung forward. "Maybe the Bridles could name the baby horse after one of the Avengers," she said, still thinking about their conversation at dinner.

"Huh?" said Lauren.

"You know. The Avengers. Iron Man, Hulk, Black Widow . . ." Lauren stared at her blankly. "Who's your favorite?" Rivka pressed.

"I don't know."

"Mine's Black Widow."

"Hmmm."

"That's *it?!* We're talking *Black Widow* here." Rivka stopped the swing and turned to face Lauren. "She's way tougher than any of the rest of them, and she doesn't need a special suit or biotech enhancement or rage or anything." This was a hot topic of debate among her siblings.

Lauren picked a hangnail and took over making them swing.

The squeal of the chain fell into a steady rhythm.

"So who'd win in a steel cage match between Captain America and Loki?" Rivka asked.

"I don't know," said the girl, chewing on her bottom lip. "I don't watch much TV."

"Comic books? Haven't you at least heard about the Avengers at school?"

Lauren shook her head. "I'm homeschooled."

"You've got to be freaking kidding me," Cat said, walking toward them from the bunkhouse with a stack of comic books in her hand. She plopped down on the swing between Rivka and Lauren. "You mean you have no idea who the Avengers even are? By the way," she said, whipping her attention to Rivka. "It's totally Loki who would win."

"No way!" Rivka shot back. "It's Cap. He's the best."

Cat rolled her eyes. "Whatever." She put the stack of comics down between them and picked up the top one—*X-Men Origins*—and started to read.

"Can I look through these?" Rivka asked.

"Sure," said Cat, not looking up. "Think that old cowgirl is going to confiscate these too?"

"Ma Etty says reading material is allowed as entertainment," Lauren offered.

Cat lowered the comic book. "Are you for real?"

"What?" said Lauren, wilting against the arm of the swing.

"Seriously. This is a ranch for *troubled* kids." She continued in a mocking tone, "'Reading material is allowed as entertainment.' What on earth could a little mouse like you have done to get stuck here?"

Lauren's expression wilted even more. It made Rivka squirm to see how uncomfortable she was. "Give it a rest, Cat," she said and handed a comic book to Lauren. "Read this one. Poison Ivy is cool."

Lauren flipped through the pages, but Rivka could tell she wasn't reading.

After a moment, she put the comic book down and said, "Cigarettes."

Rivka looked up. "What?"

"My parents caught me smoking."

Now Cat put down the comic. "You got sent to the ranch for *that*?"

Lauren dipped her chin.

"What about you?" Rivka asked Cat, remembering the breaking point in her house. Three months ago, she threw her Hebrew book across the room and followed it with a pen and a tape dispenser for good measure. The book hit her mom, and the bruise on her cheek lasted a week.

Cat waved her arm in the air as if dismissing the entire universe from her concern. "Read the report. Blah, blah, blah . . . It says carjacking. My loser stepdad sleeps with his keys now."

Rivka gaped at her. "You stole a car?"

Cat threw her hands in the air. "He's the one who taught me to drive when I was thirteen!"

"But . . ." Rivka prompted. It was obvious there was more to the story.

Cat gave a huge sigh, and her shoulders crumpled. "It doesn't matter what really happened, does it? The only thing that matters is what they think you did."

That was a lot to chew on.

"What did you do to get sent here?" Cat prodded.

Rivka pushed the swing into motion with her toe, opened her mouth, closed it again. She really didn't know how to answer that. It was everything and nothing. Maybe it was because her parents thought she was rotten to the core.

"Fine," Cat sighed. "Be that way." She forced the swing to an abrupt halt and stomped off.

Lauren stood up. "I think I'll turn in."

Rivka sat in the growing dark, not swinging. Her chest was tight. If her mom couldn't understand how that day at their synagogue affected her, no one would, especially not someone with a chip on her shoulder like Cat.

What was the point of trying to explain?

# CHAPTER SIX

It had happened last April.

Boston was emerging from winter, shedding the last of the gravel-darkened snow. Lime-colored leaves burst out of gray branches that had been bare for months. In little cracks and crannies of the pavement, dandelions poked up their little sunny heads.

Rivka loved the spring.

She loved winter too, but by February she was sick of pulling on snow boots and always wearing her parka. It was time for flip-flops and trampolines and soccer season and Passover, or as they called it in Hebrew, *Pesach*. It was her favorite Jewish holiday. Her cousins came from Providence and Baltimore to celebrate the first night of Passover with a traditional

Seder meal, and their brownstone was full of giggling and games of sardines and vases full of tulips.

The adults placed six-foot banquet tables end to end and covered them with long white tablecloths and all the things they would need for the celebration of the ancient exodus from Egypt. Things like plastic crickets and toy frogs and long strips of black cloth to simulate the plague of darkness. It was a serious holiday, but they found fun ways to reenact the story.

Rivka shouldn't even have been at the synagogue that day. Passover was celebrated at home, but the guest list had grown so long that her mother said they needed more Haggadahs—the book that led them through the prayers and stories of the Seder.

"I need you to run down to Havurah Shalom and get five more," her mother said.

Rivka was panting from a cutthroat game of hide-and-seek. "Can't Noah go?"

"I need him to move tables."

"Eli?"

Her mother gave her a hard look. "Rivka, I asked you. Take your cousin Sadie."

"Can we take the bikes?" Rivka asked. The snow had kept her from riding all winter, and she was eager for all the wheel time she could get.

Her mother smiled. "Don't forget your helmets."

She and Sadie had gone the long way through the park, and Rivka rode with her face to the sun, soaking up spring. It was marvelous. Some teenagers were slack-lining between the big oaks. A man and his dog played Frisbee. Rivka felt ready for anything.

Anything except what she saw when they rounded the last corner.

The first thing was the broken glass littering the ground in front of the synagogue. One of the tall windows that let natural light into the sanctuary was shattered. But the thing that sucked the breath out of her was the red spray paint on the carved wooden door of the synagogue.

The Nazi swastika was like a horrible, gaping wound.

Underneath it, the vandals had written *White Power* and *KKK* in huge letters.

Fear pulsed through Rivka.

She let her bike fall to the ground and clutched Sadie's hand. A crowd gathered. The rabbi came, grim-faced, and talked to the police. Several of their Muslim neighbors arrived and said that their mosque had been defaced too. Everyone looked as scared and worried as Rivka felt.

The people who did this hated her. They didn't care if she worked hard in school or tried to be a good friend. What if she had been at the synagogue when the vandals came? What would those people have done to her?

She had nightmares for weeks. She'd tried to talk to her parents but couldn't find the right words. She couldn't make them understand.

## CHAPTER SEVEN

"Time to turn in," Madison called as she left the house. Rivka heaved herself out of the swing and plodded behind her to the bunkhouse, wishing she could erase the awful memory from her brain. It hurt too much to remember.

In the cabin of the Antisocials, Madison headed into her room, singing some country song about lost love and pickup trucks. Lauren was curled up in a ball in her bottom bunk, sleeping. Or pretending to sleep. Cat was nowhere to be found, and Rivka felt relieved that she wouldn't have to face any more questions.

She changed into her pajamas, brushed her teeth, and used the bathroom.

Still no Cat.

Rivka buzzed with irritation. Just because she didn't want to talk about what had happened at home, it didn't mean Cat should get all mad at her. Where was the fairness in that?

Lights-out was supposed to be at ten. Rivka checked her watch. Fifteen more minutes. If Cat didn't feel like following the rules at the ranch, she could get in trouble all by herself. *Not my problem,* thought Rivka as she climbed into her bed.

She wasn't ready to sleep, though. Instead, she knelt on the bed and pulled back the curtain on her window. It looked out on pasture, which meant that right now it looked out on darkness. No cars rushing by. No taxis. No twenty-four-hour convenience store on the corner. Who knew what was out there? Could be anything, really.

*Well,* she corrected herself, *anything quiet.*

This was nothing like Brookline, the Boston suburb where she'd grown up.

Even B'nai B'rith camp had its share of noise. The counselors stayed up late, talking by the fire. Her brother Noah was probably there right now with his arm around some girl, listening to the motorboats *putt-putt-putting* across the lake and the faint sound of cars on the distant highway.

Madison came out to use the bathroom and saw Rivka with her forehead against the window. "Lights-out in five."

"It might be too quiet here to sleep," said Rivka.

"City girl, huh?" Madison laughed, but not in a mean way.

Rivka shrugged.

"Where's Cat?" Madison asked, suddenly noticing that the other bunk was empty.

"I haven't seen her since after dinner."

"Crap," Madison said, returning to her room. She was back in a few seconds with a fleece jacket on over her pajamas and a headlamp. She pulled on her cowboy boots and slipped out the door. Rivka heard her crunch across the gravel and head to the big house. After that, it was quiet again.

Well, almost quiet.

Barely audible sobs came from under the blankets on Lauren's bed.

Rivka watched the curve of the girl's back shudder as she cried. After a few minutes, she couldn't stand just sitting there anymore. So much for antisocial. Rivka pushed out of her bunk and went to sit at the foot of Lauren's bed.

"Hey," she said. "It's okay. First night and every-thing. Lots to get used to, right?"

Lauren pulled the blanket off her face. In the light from the open bathroom door, Rivka could see she was flushed and sweaty.

"Sorry," the girl said.

"No worries. Wanna talk about it?"

Lauren wiped her face on her sleeve. "I'm really homesick."

Rivka nodded.

"Six weeks is a long time," Lauren continued, "and every time I think about it I . . ." Her words trailed off in more sobs.

Rivka went into the bathroom and came back with a wad of toilet tissue.

Lauren sat up and blew her nose. "Where do you think Cat went?" she asked, changing the subject.

"Beats me."

"What if she doesn't come back?"

Rivka gestured to the window. "Have you looked out there? Not many places to go, if you know what I mean."

"Maybe she's hurt," Lauren suggested.

"Maybe. Wanna go look for her?"

Lauren squinted and made a thinking-hard face. "I can't sleep anyway."

The girls threw on sweatshirts and grabbed their flashlights.

Outside, the night sky was a blaze of stars. To Rivka it looked like stars on top of stars on top of stars.

Faint voices came from the big house.

The porch swing was empty.

"Maybe we should check the cars?" Lauren suggested, and the two of them walked toward the expanse of gravel where Fletch had parked the van when they arrived. It was still where they'd left it, next to a truck and a horse trailer propped up on a cinder block. There was also an old Honda Civic and a newish Ford truck, both covered with ranch dust and more than a few dents.

"Were there more cars here before?" Rivka asked.

Lauren shrugged. "I don't remember."

The girls walked around the cars looking in windows. Nothing.

"Let's look by the barn," Rivka suggested. There was something exciting about wandering in the starry dark way out in the boonies. It made her feel like an adventure could happen.

They crossed the footbridge over the creek, and once they were on the opposite side of the burbling water, Rivka began to hear a new sound. It was faint at first, but grew louder as they approached the barn.

"Is that music?" Lauren asked, wide-eyed.

Rivka nodded. "I think so."

The barn door was cracked open and a little bit of yellow light fanned out of the opening. Sure enough, from inside came the soft, plaintive sound of an old folk song. The girls tiptoed to the door and peeked in.

Paul, the ranch manager, was leaning back in an old wooden chair with his cowboy boots propped up on a hay bale and playing the harmonica. Cat sat on the stack of hay next to him with her feet tucked underneath her, listening and bobbing her head to the music.

Stalls lined either side of the barn. Sleepy horses swayed on their feet. Some poked their noses over the stall doors when Rivka and Lauren passed. Others gave a lazy flick of the tail and went back to sleep.

"Howdy, cowgirls," said Paul, lowering the harmonica. "Grab a bale."

"Madison is looking for Cat," said Lauren.

Cat scowled and continued to pick apart a piece of hay.

"I think she's worried," Rivka offered.

"I'm fine," Cat snapped. "Or I was."

Rivka held up two hands. "Just relaying the facts."

Cat started to snark back at her, but Paul interrupted.

"Okay, cowgirls, let's not get agitated. Cat and I are on lullaby duty here. One more song and then we'll go let the crew know that everyone is accounted for."

He gestured to the bales, and the girls sat. Rivka pulled up her hood so she could lean back without the hay poking her in the neck. Paul cupped the silver instrument in his hands and began to play "This Land Is Your Land." Rivka closed her eyes and let the music sway through her. Now and then a horse snuffled in the background and a bird rustled up in the rafters.

She could get used to this.

When he was done, Rivka heard quiet clapping from the door of the barn and opened her eyes to see Madison and Ma Etty leaning against the inside wall of the barn. Cat shifted uneasily next to her.

Paul grinned and raised a hand. "Found your wandering camper, Madison."

"I see that," said Madison.

"What are you all doing in here?" Ma Etty asked, walking down the barn aisle toward them, stopping now and then to scratch horse noses.

Paul tucked the harmonica into his pocket and looked a little sheepish. "Carla said that Chickpea is getting close, so I thought I might keep her company in here. Play the little mama a few lullabies before bed."

Ma Etty raised an eyebrow. "Are you going to sleep in here, Paul?"

He blushed and ran a sleeve across his face. "Give a guy a break, will you, Ma Etty?"

She beamed at him. "You can do what you like, but it's bedtime for the rest of these music lovers. Come on, ladies. Big day tomorrow."

With reluctance, Rivka, Cat, and Lauren pushed themselves off the hay bales and followed Madison to the bunkhouse. As they left the barn, Ma Etty tucked her arm into Cat's and talked with her in low whispers.

Rivka caught bits and pieces of their conversation.

*Madison was worried . . . this isn't about rules . . . taking care of each other . . . I know you know this. . . .*

Rivka wondered what it was that Cat knew. And more importantly, how she knew it.

## CHAPTER EIGHT

Immediately after breakfast the next morning, Fletch and Madison led Rivka and the other kids to the barn for their first riding lesson. If Paul had spent the night in the barn with Chickpea, he'd left no sign of it. Rivka wondered what it would be like to sleep in the creaky old building full of huge animals, with hay tickling her nose.

She went straight to Chickpea's stall to check on her.

"Baby?" Cat asked, coming up next to her.

"No baby," said Rivka, recognizing the peace offering.

Madison joined them and stroked the horse's nose. "Carla is pretty sure that it will be born while you're here."

"That would be amazing," Lauren sighed.

"Yup," the trainer agreed.

Fletch opened one of the stalls and brought out a reddish-brown horse covered with white splotches and speckles. Madison gathered the kids on the hay bales in front of him.

"This here is Sawbones," said Fletch. "He's the horse I ride. Since none of you has ever ridden before, Madison thought that a horse anatomy lesson was in order."

"Oh great," Cat murmured. "School."

Fletch nudged the horse until it stood sideways to them. "Sawbones here is a quarter horse Appaloosa mix. His color is called strawberry roan. I'm going to start here at the muzzle," said Fletch, laying his palm on the horse's nose, "and walk you through the main features."

When he put his hand on the horse's shoulder, Sawbones lifted his muzzle, opened his rubbery lips, and deftly plucked Fletch's cowboy hat right off his head.

"Hey there," said Fletch.

The horse shook the hat back and forth and then tossed it over his head so that it sailed right into Riv-ka's lap. She burst out laughing, and everyone else did too. Even Fletch. Sawbones shook his muzzle in the air like he was cracking up.

"Who's in charge of this rodeo?" Madison joked.

Fletch retrieved his hat from Rivka and settled it back on his head. "Sawbones likes to think he's a real comedian."

The horse snorted with perfect timing.

Fletch continued the lesson. Already the terms were getting mixed up in Rivka's head. So many weird ones—*pastern* and *chestnut, gaskin* and *hock.*

"Any questions?" Fletch asked.

Madison scanned their faces. "Cat?"

Rivka looked next to her. Cat had managed to tuck herself around the corner of the hay bales and had her nose in a comic book. Something with the Hulk on the cover.

"Cat!" Madison repeated, no longer smiling.

"What?"

The trainer pointed to a knobbly blob on the inside of Sawbones's knee. "What's this?"

Cat lowered the comic book and stared at the dark callus. Madison thrummed her fingers on her thigh, waiting.

"No idea," said Cat. "Scar from fighting in the zombie apocalypse?"

Madison frowned. "Cat, you are supposed to—"

Sam cut her off. "Chestnut."

All eyes flicked to him. Sam heaved himself up off the hay bales and approached the horse. With an intent look on his face, he began at one end of the horse and worked his way to the other, pointing as he named each part. "Muzzle, forehead, withers, shoulder, back, flank, barrel, point of hip, gaskin, hock, cannon, fetlock, and pastern."

Sawbones gave a little huff and nuzzled Sam's shoulder.

Fletch began the applause, a slow, deliberate clap that the others joined in.

Madison dipped her head up and down with approval. "Carla would be impressed," she said, and Sam flushed.

\\\\\\\\\\\\\\\\\\\\\\\\\\\\\\\\\\\\\\\\

At the far end of the barn, Madison introduced Rivka to a shaggy little pony named Rowdy.

"Hey," Rivka said, "I know you. You're the one who was such a piglet for grass."

"That's Rowdy, all right," said Madison, patting him on the belly. *Barrel*, Rivka reminded herself.

"He's a big chowhound, this one."

Madison showed her how to buckle on the halter, clip on a lead rope, and tie a special knot to keep him in place.

"You'll have to give him an extra-good grooming," said Madison. "He's still shedding the last of his winter coat. That's why he looks a bit like a bunny."

When Rivka stood next to Rowdy, his ears only came up to her shoulders. She scratched under long, puffy hairs that swept across his forehead like windswept bangs.

"He likes that," said Madison.

"Pretty fancy bangs for a horse," Rivka said.

"Forelock." The trainer handed her a plastic tote full of combs and brushes and showed her how to use them. "Enjoy," she said as she headed off to help Sam get to know a big brown horse two stalls down.

Rivka lifted Rowdy's forelock. Underneath, right smack in the middle of his forehead, the short, tight hair whirled into a spiral shape. It reminded her of her little brother's cowlick. The pony seemed to like it when she traced a circular pattern around the spot. He huffed softly, a sound that Madison said meant he was content.

With every pull of the curry comb, big clumps

of hair came out. Pretty soon it seemed like she had a pile of fluff big enough to make an entire bunny. She switched to a stiff brush like Madison had shown her, and when she used a fast, flicking motion, it pulled the dirt up and out of his coat. It puffed in the barn air and made her sneeze.

Rivka switched to the soft brush, and with every stroke Rowdy's coat got shinier. She hummed under her breath as she brushed, and the pony seemed almost to go to sleep. His eyes went soft, and he swayed in place slightly as she worked. Rivka was lulled by the task too. It reminded her of kneading challah for Shabbat dinner and feeling the slick dough under her palms. She stopped brushing and tossed the soft brush into the grooming tote a little too hard.

Rowdy's ears took on a backward tilt, making him look suspicious, like he expected her to throw something else. Rivka took a deep breath. "Sorry." Thinking about home was complicated, and she didn't want to do it.

"It'll be okay," Rivka told Rowdy.

For the next six weeks, her job was to think about horses.

Fletch helped Rivka find a helmet that fit and showed her how to lead Rowdy out into the arena where the others were waiting: Sam and the brown horse, Lauren with a big red one, and Cat, who stood next to a tan horse with a black mane and tail.

"Where's Sawbones?" Sam asked.

Fletch pointed out to the field, where they could see Sawbones rolling in a dusty patch of pasture. "So glad I groomed him this morning," the trainer deadpanned.

Cat gave her horse a stern look and said, "I don't want any trouble from you, Bucky."

Madison joined them in the center of the arena. "We're starting with ground work. One of the tricky things about riding is that you might not realize all the things that you're communicating to your horse."

The kids stared at her.

"Horses listen to you very carefully," Fletch added. "The way you sit in the saddle tells them as much as what you do with the reins. We start on the ground so you don't have to think of so many things at once." He demonstrated the correct way to hold the lead rope—one hand close to the clasp on the halter and the other holding the loose end of the lead rope. "Why don't you want to coil the loose end around your hand?" he asked.

"In case the horse takes off, he won't drag you with him?" Cat suggested.

Fletch gave her a thumbs-up.

"And why don't you want a bunch of loose rope dragging on the ground?" Madison asked.

Cat mimed a giant pratfall. The others laughed, and Madison said, "Exactly."

"Part of your job is to always be thinking ahead and anticipating things that can go wrong, especially things that might bother your horse," Fletch said.

"Or make your horse less responsive," said Madison. To Rivka, she added, "You would be wise to steer clear from tasty patches of grass." She pointed to the clump of grass growing at the base of the nearest fence post, and Rowdy looked longingly at it.

The trainers showed the kids how to get their horses to walk at their elbows and stop when asked. They practiced getting the horses to back up and to change directions. Rivka paid attention to Rowdy, and pretty soon she figured out that he was a lot better turning to the right than to the left, and that if she let him get within a five-foot radius of tasty green stuff, he immediately stopped listening to her and she had to get Fletch or Madison to drag him away.

After about an hour, Fletch laid out cones in

the arena, and they practiced leading their horses through the obstacle course. When they stopped for a break—lemonade for the kids and grass for the horses—Rivka sat on the fence next to Madison.

"Do they hate it?" she asked.

Madison tipped back her cowboy hat. "Does who hate what?"

"The horses. Do they hate walking around in circles like this?"

"Well, it's a little boring for them right now," Madison admitted. "But most horses like to work. They want to please you. They want to do what you ask, which is why we spend a lot of time teaching you how to ask and how to listen."

"Is that what Paul meant about *speaking horse*?"

Madison grinned at her. "Yeah, horses are herd animals. They look out for each other. To feel safe, a horse needs to know that you've got his back, that you'll stand up for him."

Rivka thought about that. She wasn't sure how a girl her age—not even thirteen—could stand up for anything.

"You're going to have your work cut out for you with Rowdy," said Madison. "He doesn't have that name for nothing."

Rivka didn't like the sound of that. "Is he mean?"

"Oh, gosh no. He's a love, but he is a pony, and that means stubborn."

"How come you gave me a horse that doesn't want to be ridden?"

Madison gave her a long, searching look. "He wants to be ridden, and he wants to have fun. Rowdy's a particularly great trail horse, but he is strong-willed. Ma Etty thought you might know something about that."

Without waiting for a response, Madison hopped down from the fence and clapped everyone else to attention. Rivka watched her and wondered exactly what it was her parents had said in their phone interview with the Bridles. It wasn't like she was stubborn or anything.

# CHAPTER NINE

After lunch, Paul hitched up the horse trailer and piled the kids into the truck. "Brace yourselves," he said. "We're going to the big city."

Main Street in the town of Quartz Creek turned out to be so short that you could miss it in the blink of an eye. When Paul pulled into the feed store parking lot, Rivka shook Sam, who had fallen asleep on the short drive from the ranch to town.

"What? Where are we?" he said, rubbing his eyes.

"You drooled," said Rivka, pointing to the shoulder of his T-shirt and wondering if he had narcolepsy or something.

"Seriously," he said, ignoring the drool comment. "When do we get to town?"

"I think this *is* town."

He peered out the window. "Cool."

"Cool?"

"Yeah. I like it."

"You slept through it."

"Through what?"

"Oh, just let me out of the truck." Rivka pushed past Sam and jumped out after Cat.

Paul gathered the kids around him. "This is chore time for today," he said. "We've got to load the trailer up with feed and bedding for the horses. If we get done in a timely manner, ice cream all around."

The thought of ice cream made Rivka's mouth water. It was a hot day, made hotter by the dust from the roads and the un-air-conditioned van. She was dreaming of mint chocolate chip when she followed Paul inside the feed store. The place was full of soft twittering noises and smelled very farmy.

"What's making that sound?" she asked Paul.

"Baby chicks," he said, pointing to six large oval-shaped metal bins at the far end of the store. Red heat lamps hung over them, making the inside of the bins glow. "Go make goo-goo eyes over 'em," said Paul. "I need to check in at the register."

Each bin was full of the cutest, tiniest balls of

fluff that Rivka had ever seen. A different variety in each bin—yellow, rusty brown, black-and-white flecked, brownish striped, black with yellow caps, and even ones with little white mohawks.

Lauren and Cat knelt on either side of Rivka and peered into the bin full of yellow chicks.

They jumped and hopped and twittered, constantly in motion, constantly making noise.

"I am going to pass out from cuteness," said Cat in a solemn voice.

"I love them so much," said Lauren, and an actual, real smile spread across her face.

Rivka reached her hand slowly into the bin. The chicks scattered, and the peeping increased to mile-a-minute.

"They probably think you're like some giant alien coming to abduct them into space," said Cat. With a smooth motion, she scooped up a chick and cradled it in two hands. It poked its fluffy head out between her fingers. Cat held it up to Rivka and made the chicken talk in a squeaky voice: "You'll never take me alive, you tentacled monstrosity! Fight, chickens, fight!"

Rivka laughed. "There should totally be a superhero chicken."

Lauren and Rivka each picked up chicks and were sitting on the floor of the feed store snuggling the babies when Carla and Paul came up. "You're never going to get them out of here now," the vet laughed.

Paul took off his cowboy hat and mopped his brow with a handkerchief. "I am doomed."

"Can we take them home?" Lauren begged. "They love us."

"Good thing Ma Etty isn't here," said Carla to Paul. "She's such a softy. You'd be going home with a box full of poultry."

Cat held up the chick in her hands. "I've already named it Turnip."

Paul held up his hands in supplication. "Can't do it, girls. Why do you think I made the feed run instead of Ma Etty? I knew that this was a den of temptation."

"Don't let them see the baby goat out back," Carla said in a pretend whisper.

The girls exploded in pleas to see the baby goat, and Paul pretended he was miffed at Carla. She laughed at him and gestured for the girls to follow. Reluctantly, they put the chicks back in the bin and headed to the lot behind the store. Sam was already there, sitting in the pen with a baby goat in his lap. He was giving it a bottle and beaming.

The little black-and-white goat was the size of a large cat. Milk leaked out of the corners of its mouth as it slurped on the oversized baby bottle. Its furry ears waggled while it drank.

"That goat is even cuter than the chicks," said Rivka.

"Give him to me," said Cat. "I wanna hold him."

Sam tightened his grip on the little goat. "He's eating."

Rivka squatted down next to Sam and scratched the goat on the head. "I am never leaving the feed store."

When the baby drained the last of the milk, Carla took him from Sam. "I told Pete, who owns the store, that I'd give the little guy a once-over," she explained and began to run her fingers over the squirmy creature.

"Why is he here?" Lauren asked. "Where's his mom?"

Rivka glanced at her. Lauren wasn't crying, for once, but she looked worried.

Carla shook her head. "He was a triplet, and his mom couldn't feed that many."

"That's really sad," said Lauren.

"It happens. But don't worry too much," she

said, scratching the baby between his ears. "This guy is in great shape, and I know a woman in town who might need a goat buddy for one of her horses."

"What would a horse want with a goat?" said Cat.

Carla looked at her for a moment. "Everybody needs a friend, right?"

Cat shrugged and seemed about to argue, but Paul gathered them up to load the trailer. "Work together," he said. "Those bags of feed weigh fifty pounds." Cat and Sam paired up, and Rivka and Lauren worked together. By the time all the supplies were stowed, Rivka and the rest were hot, sweaty, and ready for ice cream.

Paul led them down Main Street to the ice cream shop. A Formica-topped counter stretched the length of the interior. Rivka grabbed one of the round stools near the end and ordered mint chocolate chip.

While she waited for the young man behind the counter to scoop the ice cream, she scanned the flyers tacked to the announcement board on the wall. *Yoga for Cowboys* promised to add flexibility to even the most saddle-bound rangers. A handbell concert was coming at the end of June, and it wasn't too late to enter the *Famous Quartz Creek Fourth of July Parade*. Amid posters advertising the services of massage therapists, horse trainers, knife sharpeners, and tack cleaners, she saw a sign printed in crisp white letters on a red background. It said *GO HOME!*

The words, those sharp-edged letters, the way the poster was yelling at her—they made her shoulders tense, and a shiver ran through her that definitely wasn't from the air-conditioning.

Rivka lifted a flyer for banjo lessons that partially covered the rest of the sign.

*America is for Americans.*

*English Only.*

*Hey Mex—Get Out of Our Country.*

At the bottom of the sign was a call to gather and march on July 25th at four p.m.

Rivka dropped the banjo flyer, seeing in her mind the bright red spray paint on the door of her synagogue. Rivka's fists were clenched under the counter, and when the man brought her ice cream, she had to force her fingers to uncurl and take the cone. *They don't mean me*, she thought. *I'm not Mexican.* This wasn't the same as what happened at home.

"How's the mint chocolate chip?" said Paul, sliding onto the stool next to her.

"What? Um, great. Thanks," Rivka stammered.

Paul pulled on one end of his bushy mustache and peered at her like he guessed she had something on her mind. "That's good, that's good," he mused, still observing her carefully. "Are you sure you haven't hidden baby chicks in any of your pockets or anything? You look a little suspicious."

He meant it as a joke. She knew that, but something about what he said still made tears prickle behind her eyes. People really did assume the worst about other people. They figured they knew you without even knowing you. She didn't want anyone going to that stupid rally.

"Hey," Paul said, putting a hand on her shoulder. "Are you okay?"

She really might cry now.

Why did he have to be so nice?

"I was thinking about the baby goat," she stammered.

"Don't I know it," said Paul. "Wish I could have tucked the little guy in my coat pocket." He finished up his sundae and began gathering the other kids for the trip home.

Rivka finished her cone and went back to the wall of flyers with her heart pounding against her ribs. She pretended to study the announcement for a slide show on the dinosaur fossils of Colorado. As soon as she was sure no one was watching, she took down the flyer for the rally and crumpled it into a ball. On the way out of the ice cream shop, she threw it in the trash.

# CHAPTER TEN

**T**he next morning, Rivka brushed Rowdy until he gleamed, and spent ten minutes rubbing the little spiral under his bangs. She knew she was supposed to call it a forelock, but he seemed like such an eighties rocker of a pony that every time she looked at him she saw feathery, well-coiffed bangs.

"You should start a rock band," she told Rowdy. In reply, he prodded her with his nose and huffed into her ear.

"Helmet," said Madison, handing one to Rivka. "Rowdy's saddle and bridle are in the tack room. Each rack is labeled by horse."

Rivka made her way into the back room of the barn, which smelled of leather oil and horse sweat.

There were a couple of small, streamlined saddles that Fletch had said were for riding English-style, but most of them were Western saddles with a pommel at the front and tooled leather on either side. Rivka could hardly believe how much smaller Rowdy's saddle was than the one for Sam's horse.

"Are you excited?" she asked Sam.

He nodded, but didn't look up from the saddle. As Rivka watched, he tapped the saddle in a steady rhythm, starting with the pommel and working his way across the length of the saddle.

"What are you doing?" she asked, tucking her arm underneath Rowdy's saddle.

"Gotta do the parts in order."

"Huh?"

"The parts—pommel, seat, cantle, skirt, fender, stirrup, gullet . . ."

Rivka gaped at him. "How do you know that? I thought that you'd never ridden before."

"Fletch told me."

"And you memorized everything, just like that?"

"Yeah."

"That's amazing."

Sam blushed. "It's the only thing I can do right."

Rivka shifted awkwardly.

He shrugged. "My mom says it's really annoying." He hefted the saddle onto his arm and left the tack room.

For a second time, Rivka thought of her parents having their "summer off " from kids. It made her cringe to imagine the things they were probably saying about her. After their last big fight—the one where she'd said she would rather die than go through with her bat mitzvah—her mom had turned blotchy red and her voice had gone through the roof: *You are the most frustrating person I have ever known!* Her dad had sat there shaking his head, looking so disappointed. *Stubborn*, he'd said. *Why are you so stubborn?*

This is why she needed a goat buddy. *Or at least a horse buddy*, she thought, looking down at Rowdy's saddle. People were too much trouble. They never seemed to be able to get along.

\\\\\\\\\\\\\\\\\\\\\\\\\\\\\\\\\\\\\\\\\\\\\

In the arena, Fletch and Madison had them tie their horses to the crossbars of the fence and watch a demonstration. Rivka made sure to put Rowdy within reach of a tasty-looking clump of grass. She couldn't help but notice that the rest of the kids seemed to be on the same agenda as she was—stay as far away from one another as possible. They were spread out in the arena, studiously avoiding eye contact.

In the center of the arena, Madison was mounted on a black-and-white spotted horse, who pranced around, tossing its head in the air. Fletch, who was on the ground next to them, teased her. "What do you think this is, dance class?"

"You know . . ." Madison panted as she worked to get the horse calmed down, "Snow White is always a little feisty at first . . ."

"All right, cowpokes," said Fletch to the kids, "gather 'round and watch the show. This is how Madison likes to instill confidence in all y'all."

"Hey!" said Madison, reining Snow White in to stand next to Fletch. "You know what Ma Etty always says: *A challenging horse taught me everything I know.*"

Fletch tipped back his cowboy hat. "One thing you kids should know is that your summer will be filled with Ma Etty quotes. By the end, you'll be requesting T-shirts."

Madison laughed.

Fletch picked up a long, slender stick with a strip of narrow leather on the end. "This is called a carrot stick. It's not a whip. Our work at Quartz Creek Ranch is based on trust, not force. No one forces these horses to do things they don't want to do." He gave them all a long look. Rivka felt Lauren twitch like a nervous mouse next to her. "First lesson," Fletch continued, "is how to sit on your horse."

Cat snorted. "Seriously? All I get to do is sit on Bucky?"

"Seriously."

Fletch took the carrot stick and used it as a pointer to indicate Madison's ear, shoulder, hip, and heel. "See how Madison has a straight line running through her body? This is the go-to position on the horse. Her core is engaged and she's got good alignment from ear to heel. Her arms are neither too tight nor too loose." He demonstrated by pulling on the reins of the bridle. Madison's hands came forward gently and in control.

"So we're going to *sit* on our horses all day today?" Cat said. "Super exciting."

"I knew that you'd be into it," Fletch said flatly.

Madison smiled at Cat. "We're going to walk too. Watch."

The second she looked forward again, Snow White slid into an easy stride, muscles rippling under her smooth flank. The trainer and the horse looked like they were one animal. It sent a thrill through Rivka. To be understood like that would be amazing.

"How did you do that?" Cat asked.

Madison turned the horse in a circle and came to a stop in front of them. "Watch again. With horses, *small* can be much more powerful than *big* or *strong*."

"Fact is," said Fletch, "horses are always larger and stronger than you. Our communication with them should start subtle and only get bigger if they don't listen the first time."

Sam kicked at the dirt under his boots. "My dad should be on the receiving end of this lesson," he muttered. Rivka watched him out of the corner of her eye. The slump in his shoulders made her wonder about his dad and about why Sam had ended up at Quartz Creek Ranch.

"A big breath in, a slight shift of your weight forward, and a click of the tongue," Fletch was saying, "is often enough to get your horse moving."

"If that doesn't work," says Madison, "follow up with a squeeze of your legs."

She demonstrated and walked Snow White in a tight circle.

"I don't want to see any of you yelling *giddy-up*

and kicking your horse in the barrel," Fletch admonished. "You are not in a made-for-TV Western!"

"I like movies," Sam said without looking up from the dirt.

Madison swung down from her horse, and she and Fletch showed Lauren and Cat how to mount up. After that, it was Rivka's turn. Up on Rowdy's back, Rivka felt kind of dorky. Her long legs curved around his fat little belly and felt almost like they would skim the dirt. He stood stolidly, and Rivka got the distinct impression that he expected this to be the dreariest part of his day. That gave her a pang of sadness.

She wanted to be fun.

She really did.

Being the problem child wasn't all it was cracked up to be.

"Rivka?" Madison patted her on the knee. "Hello in there. Anybody home?"

She shook her head and twitched on Rowdy's back. "Sorry. Wandering."

Madison tilted her head to one side and looked at her with concern. "I see that. Are you okay?"

"Sure. Yeah."

"Okay," the trainer said with a gentleness that

Rivka imagined her using with a hurt dog or a heartbroken child. Madison gave her knee a squeeze. "I need you to stay focused up there. Otherwise, it stresses Rowdy out."

Rivka nodded. "Got it. Don't stress out the pony."

Madison took a step back and appraised Rivka's form. "You've got a good natural seat," she told Rivka. "You sit tall. Not stiff like a board, but no slouch. Perfect."

Rivka smiled at her and lifted her hands, holding the reins. "What do I do with these?"

Madison adjusted Rivka's grip on the reins and then took hold of the thin leather straps and tugged on them. "You want to keep this amount of tension between you and Rowdy. If you stiffen up and jerk on his mouth, he will refuse to move for you. He's stubborn that way."

"But if he's stubborn, don't I have to be tough with him?"

Madison looked up at her. "That seems logical, doesn't it?"

Rivka shrugged.

"Well," her trainer continued, "what you have to do is learn to speak horse."

"That's what Paul said."

"Smart man," Madison said. "There are two common mistakes people make when riding. The first is giving mixed messages to the horse."

"I don't understand."

"Like pressing in with your heels, which means *Let's get going*, and leaning back, which means *Slow it down*. Mixed messages."

Rivka chewed on that idea. Mixed messages were like her father suggesting that she *think about the bat mitzvah* when he really meant *You have to do it* or her mother saying that nothing bad would happen to her at their synagogue when Rivka knew that was a lie.

"What's the other mistake?" Rivka asked.

"Yelling," said Madison.

Rivka frowned. "People do that? They just scream at their horses?"

Madison smiled. "Not like you're thinking. Yelling at a horse is when you give them an instruction and then keep giving it louder and louder and louder. In other words, say you want your horse to turn, so you pull on the reins. And then each time you keep pulling harder and harder. That's yelling."

"So I pull, but then what?"

"You're a smart one," the trainer said with a grin. "I can tell."

Rivka grinned back.

"You give a tug and then relax as soon as the horse starts to respond. Your job is to really pay attention to what the horse is saying back." Madison let that sink in. "Ready to give it a go?" she asked.

"I guess so," said Rivka.

"Perfect!" The trainer traced a wide circle in the air with one finger. "Take a lap around the arena. Strong seat. Start subtle. Listen to your horse."

Rivka took a deep breath, suddenly panicked by how much there was to remember. She leaned forward and pressed her calves against the pony's sides.

Nothing.

"You're holding the reins too tightly," said Madison. "Let your arms be like a rubber band, stretch with him."

Rivka tried again. Breathe, lean, squeeze. At the last moment she remembered that she should also make that clicking sound with her tongue. She did it and, lo and behold, Rowdy hopped into a perky little walk.

Madison crowed. "Awesome! Achievement unlocked! You are on your way to being fluent in horse!"

## CHAPTER ELEVEN

**B**y the end of the lesson, Rivka was mentally and physically exhausted. She collapsed into the porch swing next to Cat. "There are so many different things to think about all at the same time. My brain hurts."

Cat was sweaty and sunburned. When she lifted her sunglasses, she looked like a raccoon. "My legs are noodles. They will never recover."

Sam joined them on the porch steps. "You were all like, *We're just going to sit on our horses?! How hard could that be?*" His impression of Cat from the beginning of the lesson was spot on.

"Oh, shut up," said Cat, too wiped out to put up more of a fight.

Lauren came out of the big house with a pitcher of lemonade in one hand and a tower of glasses in the other. Rivka took the cups, and Sam pulled a small table over. They sat in silence, quenching their thirst and watching a couple of chickens peck their way across the lawn. It was almost lunchtime, and the sun was straight overhead. A few bees lazily circled the roses climbing up the porch. The horses in the pasture chewed mouthfuls of grass in slow motion. There was hardly any breeze. Not even the leaves on the trees seemed inclined to move.

Rivka caught a glimpse of a cloud of dirt way down Bridlemile Road and watched as it resolved into a pickup truck rumbling toward them. It clattered through the arched gateway of the ranch and braked in front of the house. Dust billowed around the beat-up truck in the dry air. Three men who had been packed shoulder to shoulder in the cab piled out. Even though it was hot, they were wearing jeans and long-sleeved flannel shirts, and handkerchiefs knotted around their necks. The man who had been driving tipped his cowboy hat back on his head and approached the kids.

"Buenos días," he said. "I am looking for Paul, the manager here." His accent gave the words a smooth, rolling lilt.

The two men behind him scuffed their boots in the gravel and exchanged a few words in Spanish. After two hours of paying super-close attention to Rowdy, Rivka read the nervousness that came off of them like they were speaking horse. The sense that something was wrong made her suddenly alert.

"I'll get him," she said while the others were still staring open-mouthed.

"Gracias," said the first man who had spoken.

Last time she had seen Paul, he was checking on Chickpea. The pregnant horse was standing in her stall, half asleep, but there was no sign of Paul or his giant mustache. Rivka checked the tack room. Empty. She heard some kind of banging out back and went to check behind the barn. Sure enough, there he was. Or, at least, she thought that was Paul, half obscured by the engine of a big piece of farm equipment.

"Knock, knock," she said, coming up next to the tractor.

"Hang on. Gotta tighten this down."

Rivka heard the sound of a tool on metal, grunting, and a rusty screech.

"Got it!" said the ranch manager, emerging from the metal guts of the machine. "Well, hey there, cowgirl! How was your lesson? You and Rowdy BFFs yet?"

Rivka grinned at him. "Not yet, but we're getting there."

"Good, good. What brings you back here to my office?"

"There are some men here to see you."

Paul raised a bushy blond eyebrow. "Is it the law?"

It took a moment for Rivka to realize he was joking. "No. Nothing like that. But it looks serious. These guys seem upset."

Paul's humor vanished. He wiped engine grease off his hands. "Okay then. Let's go."

She trailed him around the barn and back to the porch. Lauren had given the three men lemonade, and they were drinking in silence.

"Hola, amigos," said Paul, striding forward with his hand extended. "¿Qué pasa?"

The men shook hands all around and began speaking in rapid-fire Spanish. Rivka couldn't follow any of it, but she watched their faces. Paul's perpetual grin faded, and soon he looked as serious as the other men. After about five minutes, the men shook hands again and headed for the truck. Right before the driver closed the door, he called back to Paul, in English this time. "You'll tell Señor Bridle, yes?"

"Absolutely," said Paul in a low, heavy voice. "Take care."

When the truck was gone, Cat set down her lemonade glass with a bang and stood. "That looked like serious drama. What's going on?"

Paul sighed. "Nothing for you guys to worry about." But immediately, Rivka felt uneasy.

"You know," said Sam, pulling a piece of string out of his pocket and tying it into an intricate series of knots, "when adults say stuff like that, all it does is make us worry more."

"We can handle the truth," said Cat. "We're tough." She had her hands on her hips and her chin jutted forward. Rivka thought she looked almost as tough as Black Widow.

Paul patted her on the shoulder. "I know you are."

Sam unraveled the knots in his string and began retying them. "You'd better tell us because Cat won't let you off the porch if you don't."

Paul pulled off his cowboy hat and wiped his forehead on his sleeve. "A friend of ours, a young man who swims with Madison, he ran into a bit of trouble in town last night."

"And . . ." Cat prodded.

"He was jumped coming home from the pool. Got pretty messed up."

"He got beat up? Why?" Lauren asked in a worried voice.

Paul let out another big sigh. "Elias is from Mexico. Seems like that might have had something to do with it."

Rivka stared at her hands, remembering the words *White Power* on the synagogue door, and then the flyer in the ice cream shop. It made her stomach hurt. Coming to Colorado was supposed to be different.

\\\\\\\\\\\\\\\\\\\\\\\\\\\\\\\\\\\\\\\\\\\\

Rivka was still out of sorts after chore time.

She and Sam had been assigned to pull weeds in the garden. He weeded on his knees with his nose inches from the plants, and he only pulled one kind of weed at a time before going back through the row removing a second kind of weed. All he said by way of explanation was, "Single search image maximizes efficiency," and since Rivka had no idea what that meant, she focused on getting her row of tomatoes into tip-top shape.

The mindless task left a little too much time for thinking.

When all the chores were finished, no one could decide what to do.

"Croquet is stupid," Cat announced when Lauren suggested it.

Sam held out his piece of rope. "Wanna learn to tie some knots?"

Lauren bit her lip and went back to hunting through the shed of games.

Rivka joined her. "How about corn hole?" she suggested, pulling out the slanted board with target holes in it.

Lauren held out a racket. "Badminton?"

Rivka and Lauren set up the badminton net on the grass in front of the bunkhouses.

Cat micromanaged from the hammock. "That's too slumpy. Tighten up the left side." Lauren adjusted the stakes. "No, wait. That's too much. Now it's crooked."

Lauren's hands balled into fists, and her face turned bright red. "Are you even going to play?" she snapped.

Cat smirked at her. "Maybe."

"Frattleprat!" Lauren spat.

Sam looked up from his knots. "What in the . . . ?"

"Frattleprat?" Cat repeated, a look of disbelief on her face.

Rivka could feel Lauren turn rigid.

She kind of wanted to see her blow a gasket. Cat deserved it, but instead, Rivka put a hand on Lauren's shoulder. "Let it go. I'll play with you."

Lauren's nostrils pinched together as she sucked in a breath. "My parents don't let me swear," she said, holding her racket in a death grip.

"Hey," said Cat, jumping out of the hammock, completely oblivious to the fact that Lauren wanted to use her for a birdie. "I've got a better idea."

The others watched, open-mouthed, as Cat dragged the corn hole board to the far side of the net, grabbed a handful of beanbags, and returned to the hammock. Once she had got herself swinging, Cat began chucking the beanbags over the net toward the corn hole board. The first one was way off. The second fell short. The third smacked the board and slid through one of the holes.

"Wa-hoo!" Cat shrieked. "Look at me go!"

Pretty soon, they'd made up a bunch of rules and were all wrestling to get prime position in the hammock. They tossed beanbags and screamed

"Frattleprat!" whenever they missed the target holes on the board. It was mayhem.

Mayhem that ended when Madison got home from swimming laps at the public pool in town.

When she parked the truck, they could tell that she'd been crying.

Rivka, Cat, and Lauren followed her into the bunkhouse. When they asked her about Elias, all she would say was that it would be a long time before he would swim again. Then she went into her room and shut the door.

The rest of the Antisocials read comic books until dinner. No one felt much like talking.

## CHAPTER TWELVE

The next morning, when they went to the barn to saddle the horses, they found Paul sleeping in a pile of hay next to Chickpea's stall.

"Rise and shine, sleeping beauty," said Madison, nudging him awake.

The bleary-eyed ranch manager mumbled into his sleeve and went back to snoring.

Madison shook him again. "Paul, wake up."

"Chickpea?!" he said, sitting up.

She shook her head. "Nothing yet."

He groaned.

"Go get some sleep," Madison told him. "We'll keep an eye on her."

Too tired to protest, Paul stumbled to the

hammock and went back to sleep. Throughout riding lessons, either Madison or Fletch kept popping back into the barn to check on the horse. She was pacing more and seemed agitated. Everyone felt sure that the baby was coming soon. For the rest of the day, that was all anyone could talk about. What if the foal was born in the middle of the night? Would it be a filly or a colt? What would they name it?

At dinnertime, Paul and Ma Etty made plates for themselves and ate in the barn.

Sam was washing dishes, Cat was rinsing, and Rivka was drying when Paul charged through the front door.

"It's time," he panted.

Mr. Bridle carefully folded the newspaper he had been reading and stood while Paul did a nervous jig on the front mat. Mr. Bridle stood and patted Paul on the shoulder. "Easy there. Chickpea has done this before. She knows what to do."

Paul tugged on his mustache. "Can you call Carla?"

The old man nodded, and Paul sprinted back to the barn.

Rivka stacked the last plate and hung up the dish towel.

"Do we get to watch?" Cat asked, her hands on her hips.

"If you want to," Mr. Bridle said as he walked to the office.

Cat gave an emphatic nod. "Cool."

"Will it be slimy?" Lauren asked.

"If it's anything like a human baby, it will be a total goo-fest," said Cat.

Rivka cocked her head. "Have you seen a baby being born?"

Cat held up three fingers.

"Seriously?" Rivka gaped at her.

She made a face. "Unfortunately."

"How?" Rivka asked, remembering the other day when Cat had said she didn't like babies, at least not human babies.

Cat's expression turned even more sour. She ticked the babies off her fingers like they were maladies. "My brother Jonas was born at home with a midwife while I watched *My Little Pony* on cable. I was at the hospital with Mom when my sister, Sloane, popped out. And best of all . . ." The scorn in her voice made Rivka wince. "Jack was born on a city bus. So when you ask about slime," she said, turning to Lauren, "let me tell you, they won't ever get that bus seat clean."

"Ew!" said Lauren.

"Why was he born on a bus?" asked Rivka.

Cat shrugged. "He came really fast. It was horrible."

"Everybody ready for a horse birth?" said Mr. Bridle, returning from the office and clapping his hands expectantly.

The girls exchanged glances. Lauren bit her lower lip and looked ready to bolt. Rivka was rethinking her plan too, but Sam swept past them.

"Come on, you big wusses," he said. "Pretend it's a biology lesson."

Rivka fell in behind him, and the entire crew walked to the barn in the growing dusk. The sun had set behind the row of purple mountains, but the sky still glowed with evening light. The horses were being left out in the pasture tonight, partially because it was so warm and lovely, but also so that Chickpea could have the barn to herself. Rivka caught sight of Rowdy clustered with the others at the near end of the pasture. Someone had thrown them a few extra flakes of alfalfa. He seemed to be enjoying dessert.

"Low voices. No quick movements," Mr. Bridle reminded them as they slipped through the door of the barn.

Chickpea was in the double-sized stall at the end of the barn. Paul and Ma Etty stood on hay bales on either side of the door and leaned against the walls of the stall, looking over. Silently, Ma Etty gestured to them, and Rivka and Cat climbed up next to her. The horse was standing in the middle of the stall with her legs splayed. Ma Etty had wrapped Chickpea's tail so that the long pale hairs were out of the way. Chickpea's head hung very low, and she swayed slightly.

Rivka might be a beginner at speaking horse, but even she could tell that the horse was deeply focused and in pain. When she had imagined this moment, Rivka had pictured Ma Etty sitting near the horse's head and talking to her. Maybe saying *Breathe, breathe, push,* like they do in the movies. But actually, she realized that Ma Etty was doing the best thing by letting Chickpea work through labor in her own way.

A shudder went through the pregnant horse. Rivka winced. It was hard to watch her struggle like this. Chickpea circled the stall, plodding through the thick, fresh straw Paul had spread for her. She was panting and breathing hard. Her huge belly undulated.

"Ugh. Creepy," said Cat. "It's like in *Alien*."

Rivka made a disgusted face. Noah had let her watch that movie last summer when their parents had gone out for the night. He got grounded for a week. She'd had nightmares for far longer.

"How long does it usually take?" she whispered to Ma Etty.

"Once things really get moving, not very long."

Chickpea's wrapped tail lifted slightly. Underneath it, Rivka could see a bluish-white membrane, like a partially filled water balloon, emerging from what she could only guess was the birth canal.

Lauren looked like she might pass out.

Cat gave a low whistle. "What the heck?"

"Amniotic sac," Ma Etty whispered. "Watch for the forelegs next."

Rivka felt twitchy. The horse looked so unhappy, and it seemed impossible for a full-sized foal to come out of there. She wrapped her arms tightly around herself.

Ma Etty leaned into her. "You okay?"

"What if something goes wrong? Carla's not here yet."

The old woman slung her arm around Rivka's shoulder and squeezed. "It's going to be okay.

Chickpea hardly ever needs help when she foals, and besides, I've delivered a few in my time."

"You can help her?" Rivka pressed.

"If she needs me, I can. And Paul and Mr. Bridle too. But look . . ."

Two tiny hooves were visible in the milky sac.

Chickpea circled again, huffed, and made a slow-motion fall to the ground.

Rivka and Cat gasped. "Is she okay?" they said together.

Ma Etty's face was serious, but she nodded yes, never taking her eyes off of the horse's rear end.

Rivka clutched Ma Etty's hand. "How do you know?" she asked. "How can you be sure?"

The older woman tilted her chin toward the horse. With a grunt, Chickpea shifted her body, and the hooves emerged farther. Tucked in between the spindly little legs, Rivka could make out the rounded muzzle of the foal. She held her breath. All around her the others waited, frozen in place. Every eye was on the horse. Rivka wasn't thinking about the slime or the grossness or anything except that teeny, tiny foal pushing its way into the world.

With a violent thrashing of her legs in the straw, Chickpea pushed again, and the foal's head and forelegs were out, clearly visible through the sac that still enclosed it.

"It's not moving," Rivka stammered. "Why isn't it moving?"

Ma Etty patted her arm. "It's okay. The foal is still attached to the placenta."

Rivka felt someone come up behind them.

It was Carla. "How's she doing?" she asked in a quiet voice.

"Really great," said Ma Etty.

Paul waved Carla over, and she squeezed onto the hay bale between him and Lauren. Rivka watched him slide an arm around her waist as she settled in to watch.

Chickpea was breathing hard. Her sides heaved, and for a few minutes nothing happened. No one moved. Then once again, Chickpea's flanks began to tremble, and her legs pawed at the straw. The horse gave one more huge push, and the rest of the foal emerged in a quivering mass of slime and membrane and pink-tinged fluid.

Rivka exhaled loudly.

The horse dropped her head on the straw and lay there, motionless.

Carla stepped off the hay bale and entered the stall carefully. "There, there, Chickpea. Good girl.

Good girl," she murmured, running one hand softly down her length. With deft hands, she pulled the membrane away from the foal's head. Carla stood back.

The baby, a soft yellow like its mom, lifted its head.

Chickpea lifted her head and looked back at it.

Their noses twitched.

Rivka thought she would explode with happiness.

The still-wet baby was gawky and uncoordinated, but it untangled its legs and sat up. Chickpea stood and began to nudge the baby to its feet. The tiny creature struggled to coordinate all four legs, wobbling and tottering, while Chickpea nosed and licked her baby.

It was the most miraculous thing Rivka had ever seen.

A rushing sensation filled her. This was magic. Better than magic. Rivka was all sparkly inside. She didn't mean to sing, but she couldn't help it. The prayer bubbled out of her. A hum at first, then the ancient Hebrew words took shape in a quiet melody—*shehecheyanu vekiymanu vehigi'anu lazman hazeh*. She didn't realize the others were even listening until Paul let out a low whistle of appreciation.

"That was beautiful," said Mr. Bridle.

"What does it mean?" asked Lauren.

"It's . . . um . . ." Suddenly Rivka was embarrassed. "It's a Jewish prayer. You say it when you experience something amazing for the first time."

Mr. Bridle put his hands on her shoulders. "Thank you, Rivka. Thank you for singing."

Chickpea bent her body around the foal, and it began to nurse.

For a long time they all watched the mother and baby.

Finally, Carla roused herself. She gave Paul a hug. "I told you she would be fine. Shall we see who wins our little bet?"

Paul waggled his mustache at her. "Colt," he challenged.

"We'll see."

Carla and Ma Etty went in together. The older woman went straight to Chickpea, stroking her muzzle and talking to her quietly. The vet ran her hands over the foal. As soon as she was done, she gestured for Ma Etty, and they left the stall.

"So?" Paul prompted.

Carla gave him a mischievous grin. "Perfectly healthy . . . foal."

He groaned in mock despair. "You must be the world's worst vet if you can't even tell that it's a—"

She interrupted him. "Colt. It's a colt."

"Ha! I told you so!"

Carla laughed, and Ma Etty shook her head. "He's incorrigible. What on earth did you bet, Carla?"

"Loser buys dinner. So dumb."

Paul rubbed his stomach in an exaggerated circle. "I'm already hungry."

"It's getting late, team," said Mr. Bridle.

Ma Etty peered at Mr. Bridle's wrist to check his watch. "Almost ten," she said, shooing Rivka and the other kids out of the barn. "Off to bed with you."

"What about the baby?" Rivka asked. "Who's keeping an eye on him?"

Ma Etty glanced over her shoulder. Paul and Carla were sitting close to each other on the hay bale by Chickpea's stall. "Looks like the nighttime watch is in place. Don't you worry about a thing."

Rivka yawned and followed Lauren and Madison to the bunkhouse.

Their boots crunched on gravel. Somewhere down the creek, an owl broke into a raucous tremolo. The frogs in the pasture pond chirruped and sang. After the others had gone inside, Rivka paused on the porch and looked up at the sky and felt like she might drift up into the darkness, where it was nothing but stars upon stars. Her heart pulsed in time with them. Remembering the little colt's velvet nose and his big eyes and his mother's tender care, she felt dizzy. It was almost like she could feel the galaxy spinning.

# CHAPTER THIRTEEN

**W**ith permission from Ma Etty, Rivka ducked out of breakfast early the next morning to check on Chickpea and the baby. When Rivka got to the barn, the new arrival was curled up in a little ball in the straw, almost like a dog. Overnight his coat had dried into yellow fuzz. His tail was only about six inches long and covered with downy white fluff that looked soft as cotton.

The colt still didn't have a name.

Ma Etty had said they could all make suggestions.

Sam was already on a roll of completely terrible names, including Potato Chip, Slimer, and Dump Truck.

That last one didn't even make sense.

Rivka had to come up with something perfect. The colt needed a name that captured how marvelous he was. Maybe Dreamer or Thunder.

When Fletch got out to the barn to give the horses their morning grain, he called Rivka into the tack room. He showed her the whiteboard where each horse's breakfast requirements were listed, and put her to work measuring grain and adding supplements as needed. She liked the work, and she liked the attentive way Fletch went about his own tasks. She watched him take a moment with each horse, stroking its neck or scratching behind its ears.

She liked Fletch. He knew what to focus on.

When she heard the others outside the barn door, she hurried to grab Rowdy's halter and rope. She was eager to get riding. Madison was in the pasture, rounding up Snow White. When she saw Rivka, she held up one hand and asked her to wait by the gate.

She led the black-and-white horse toward Rivka, and several other horses followed, including Rowdy. "Morning," she said. "Got his stuff?"

Rivka held up the halter and rope.

Madison nodded and opened the gate to let her in. "Do you remember how that goes on?"

"I think so." Rivka slid the halter over Rowdy's

nose and settled the strap behind his ears. She buckled it near his cheek and clipped the lead rope onto the lower ring of the halter. The others came out to retrieve their horses for lesson time, and they led the horses to the arena.

"We'll groom them out here," Madison said, tying Snow White to the fence, "so that Chickpea and the baby can have some peace and quiet."

Rivka got Rowdy's grooming tote and began to curry the dirt out of his coat. "Have you been rolling around in the mud?" she asked him. He huffed at her and swished his tail. "You deny it," she said, "but what about this?" Rivka used her fingernail to scrape off a chunk of dried mud stuck to Rowdy's neck. "Guilty as charged!" she announced, switching brushes.

When Rowdy was dirt-free, Madison supervised as Rivka saddled and bridled him, offering suggestions when Rivka wasn't sure what to do. Then Madison held Rowdy's head, and Rivka mounted.

"Heels down a bit more," the trainer suggested. Rivka adjusted. When Madison was satisfied with her alignment, she asked her to make several warmup circles in the arena.

At first things went without a hitch.

Rivka asked Rowdy to go using the inclination

of her body, the click of her tongue, and a squeeze of her heels. He set off at a bouncy walk, and instantly she was focusing on all the things she needed to remember—steady tension in her arms, chin lifted, a tightness to her abdominal muscles.

On the first circle, she barely noticed Sam when she passed him, but on the second circle, he and his horse settled in next to her. "You ate bacon at breakfast the other day."

"So?"

"So," he repeated. "I thought you were Jewish. Isn't that illegal or something?"

Annoyance billowed through her. She hated the bacon question. Rowdy sensed her irritation and balked, taking a few steps in the direction of some particularly tasty-looking grass. She hurried to put her attention in the right place, course-correcting before he got within snack distance.

"My family doesn't keep kosher," she said.

"And aren't you supposed to wear a hat thing?" Sam pressed. "Or is that only for guys?"

Rivka wanted to scream. Sometimes she felt like everyone in the world learned about Jews from *Fiddler on the Roof.* Next thing, Sam would be asking about matchmakers.

"I'm trying to ride here," she snapped. "And it's called a kippah or a yarmulke and I don't wear one outside of synagogue, okay?"

He held up his hands, and his horse halted.

Rivka gave Rowdy a jab in the ribs with her heels so she could get away. She was mad, and she kicked harder than she meant to. The pony jumped into a startled trot, and Rivka had to clutch at the pommel to stay in the saddle.

"Easy there," Madison called. "You need to rein him in."

Rivka fumbled at the reins and asked Rowdy to stop. She did that too hard as well, and the pony tugged back, jerking the reins from her hand. Madison was beside her now, taking ahold of the reins under Rowdy's chin. "What's going on here?"

"Tell Sam to leave me alone," Rivka shot back.

Madison looked steadily into her face. "Sam is working with Fletch now. You need to get your focus back."

"He's the problem, not me."

Madison tipped her cowboy hat. "Time for a break."

"I don't need a break."

"I say you do."

"I'm fine," Rivka snapped.

The trainer squinted at her. "Then you need to pull it together. Breathe."

Rivka breathed. She was still irritated, but at least Madison let go of Rowdy's bridle.

"I want you to walk Rowdy around the arena twice," she said.

Rivka nodded. This time Rowdy responded. On the second loop around the arena, Cat rode up next to her. "We could name the foal Peanut. Or Sandman."

"I doubt the Bridles will go for that."

"You might be right," Cat mused, apparently not noticing Rivka's sour mood. "They're not comic book people. They probably don't even realize that they named my horse after Bucky Barnes."

A moment later she said, "Are you doing one of those bar mitzvah thingies?" Rivka pressed her heels into Rowdy's sides to make him speed up, but he refused, remaining nose-to-nose with Cat's horse. "It's kind of like a really huge birthday party plus church, right?"

"No," Rivka said, through clenched teeth.

Cat shot her a side-eye. "Well, what is it then?"

"It's called a bat mitzvah for girls, and no, I'm not having one." Her voice went up a notch.

"Why not?"

"Why do you care?"

Cat stared at her like she'd grown three heads. It made Rivka want to throw something.

"It's called conversation," she muttered. "Chill out."

But Rivka couldn't chill out. Every time someone asked her about something Jewish, it dredged up what had happened at the synagogue. It was the last thing in the world Rivka wanted to think about.

"You don't have a clue what you're talking about," she spluttered. "Hebrew is boring, and the tutor is a freaky old witch, and my brother is the perfect one, not me!" She kicked Rowdy hard to try to get him to move away from Cat. It had the exact opposite effect. The pony stopped in his tracks.

Madison raced over and grabbed ahold of Rowdy. "Get off the horse," she snapped.

Rivka dismounted and jerked away from Madison.

"Stay out of my business," she yelled, glaring at Madison and Cat and the rest of them. "Leave me alone!" Then Rivka stomped out of the arena.

# CHAPTER FOURTEEN

**M**a Etty came into the bunkhouse without knocking. Her gray curls were pinned up over her ears on either side, and she was wearing a T-shirt that said *May the Horse Be With You.*

"You missed lunch," she said, leaning against the door frame.

Rivka shrugged and went back to the card house she was building on the table.

"Hungry?"

Rivka shrugged again.

"You need to come with me."

Now Rivka met the old woman's eyes. Ma Etty's face was placid—kind, even. Nothing like her mother's was when Rivka was in trouble.

"Where are we going?"

"I need your help with a job in town."

"What about chores and free time?"

Ma Etty shook her head. "I need you to stick with me."

"I don't want to go to town."

It was Ma Etty's turn to shrug. "This afternoon will give you some time to consider what happened in the arena." She held the door open and gestured for Rivka to get moving.

There was a sandwich wrapped in waxed paper on the passenger seat of the truck. Rivka ate it as they rumbled along the dirt road. She kept expecting a lecture, but Ma Etty fiddled with the radio dial and tuned in to a station with lots of accordion music that sounded almost like polkas, but the songs were in Spanish. The old woman didn't explain where they were going, and Rivka didn't ask.

Half an hour later, they pulled to a stop in front of a church.

Rivka snuck a glance at the old woman. What was she up to?

She followed Ma Etty around the back of the church. A set of sunken concrete steps led to the door of the lower level. Inside were half-full racks of clothes on hangers, and bins labeled with things like *0–6 months* and *toddler* and *boys' pants size 6–8*.

"Everything is organized by size," said Ma Etty. Gesturing to a pile of cardboard boxes and black garbage bags brimming with clothes, she explained, "We need to sort these donations. If there is anything that doesn't seem clean, we'll wash it." Ma Etty directed her attention to the washer and dryer on the far wall. "Okay," she said. "Let's get to it."

Rivka opened the first bag. Musty-smelling old-man sweaters. Size large. Ma Etty handed her some hangers and showed her where on the racks they belonged. After that, Rivka sat down in the corner with a box full of baby clothes and folded onesies into small piles. It was enough to make her hate babies too.

She was going to have to apologize to Cat.

She knew that.

Community service was a big part of the whole bar and bat mitzvah thing. Making the world a better place and all that. Ma Etty was way too much like Rivka's rabbi back home, and her punishment couldn't have been more obvious. Ma Etty didn't have to spell it out. Rivka spent the afternoon sorting T-shirts and hanging up girls' dresses. She folded clean laundry that came out of the dryer. It was boring and sometimes gross, like the smelly bag of boys' gym shorts she had to deal with.

But it was brainless.

That was good.

She zoned out. Fold, crease, stack. And no one talked to her. A woman in a paramedic's uniform arrived to help.

"Howdy, Marisol," said Ma Etty. "You look like you're coming from work."

"On my way, actually," the woman said in a beautiful Mexican accent. "I have an hour before my shift starts."

Their talk turned to the young man, Elias, and as much as Rivka didn't want to listen, she couldn't help but hear.

"I was working when the call came in," said Marisol, shaking her head sadly. "Poor Elias. He was in bad shape."

"Is he going to be okay?" Ma Etty asked.

Marisol nodded. "Physically, yes, but I don't know about the rest. His whole family is talking about going back to Jalisco. The younger children are scared."

Ma Etty clucked in dismay. "That's terrible. Do you really think they'll leave?"

Marisol's frown deepened. "I don't know."

"I hope not. This is their home. And besides," Ma Etty said, "few of the cattle ranches in this valley could function without their Mexican and Peruvian ranch hands. These guys know their horses."

"But what about that rally?" Marisol asked.

Ma Etty put her arm around the woman's shoulders. "We'll stick together like we always do."

As they talked, Rivka shrank into herself. She didn't want to hear about this. She wanted to burrow into the pile of clothes and disappear. It was starting to seem like it wasn't safe anywhere.

\\\\\\\\\\\\\\\\\\\\\\\\\\\\\\\\\\\\\\\\\

When they got back to the ranch, Madison rushed to Ma Etty's side. "We've got a problem."

The sight of her flushed, worried face set Rivka's pulse racing.

"Do you want to fill me in now or in private?" Ma Etty asked calmly, tilting her head to indicate Rivka.

"She's gonna know one way or another."

Ma Etty nodded her agreement.

"Cat's wandered off again," Madison explained, the words rushing out of her. "We haven't seen her since lunchtime. Mr. Bridle and Paul are riding the fence lines in the ATVs. I've got the kids here looking. Fletch thinks it's time to call in Sheriff Handy."

Rivka followed Madison and Ma Etty up the porch steps and inside the ranch house, but her limbs were leaden. Her mouth tasted sour. Cat was gone. Her apology was too late.

"Did she take a horse?" Ma Etty asked.

Madison shook her head. "I checked the barn. Her saddle and bridle are there. Bucky is in the pasture."

"Cars are all accounted for?"

Rivka remembered the way Cat had said *blah, blah, blah . . . carjacking.*

But Madison pulled a handful of key rings from her pocket. "Nothing's gone, and I'm holding all the extra keys."

"Good thinking." Ma Etty pursed her lips and looked at Rivka. "Any ideas?"

She swallowed hard. Asking where Cat might be felt almost accusatory. *Where is she? Shouldn't you know? This is your fault.* She laced her fingers and unlaced them and shoved them in her pockets. "I really have no idea. Maybe someplace obvious."

"Obvious?" Ma Etty prompted.

"I don't know," Rivka stammered. "Is she asleep in the hammock? Did you check the chicken coop?"

"Of course we did," Madison snapped, and Rivka shrank back.

Ma Etty took the handful of keys from Madison. "Can you double-check the bunkhouses, the hammock, and the chicken coop?"

Madison's lips squeezed into a tight line. "I've done that."

"I'm sure you have," said Ma Etty, patting her arm. "One more time for me, though. I'm going to call the neighbors, and I'll give Sheriff Handy a heads-up."

When Madison was gone, Rivka asked, "What do you want me to do?"

Ma Etty looked at her watch. "It's almost 6:30. The horses need to be fed. Can you do that?"

"I helped Fletch in the morning once. What each horse needs is on the whiteboard, right?"

"Exactly," said Ma Etty, looking grateful. "All you have to do is put the food in the grain bins in each stall. I will bring the horses in as soon as I'm done making calls."

As she walked across the bridge to the barn, Rivka wondered whether or not Cat might have tried to walk into town. It was awful—not knowing where she was and not being able to apologize. If only she hadn't lost her temper . . .

The barn was quiet except for a few birds in the rafters. Rivka went into the tack room and turned on the light. She measured out Rowdy's dinner first and added his mineral supplement. She poured it into the grain bucket in his stall, made sure his water was full, and tossed a flake of hay on the ground.

Next she measured out dinner for Sawbones and Snow White.

Rivka worked her way down the list in the tack room, making sure that each horse had what it needed. Like folding the clothes in the church basement, the work calmed her frayed nerves, and all the numbers—cups of grain, scoops of probiotics, flakes of hay—didn't leave room for her to worry about Cat or Elias or what would happen when she had to go back home.

Last of all, Rivka prepared Chickpea's meal.

Carla had written up a detailed list of supplements for the new mama.

While Rivka scooped and measured, she tried to think of a good name. It was kind of dumb that they were still calling him *the baby*. Maybe they should just name him *Baby* and be done with it. *Or Phil*, she thought. *He kind of looks like a Phil.*

When she got to the stall, he was nursing.

Chickpea nuzzled her baby's flank while he fed.

"I've got your dinner too," Rivka told her, opening the stall door to slip inside and fill the grain bin.

She found more than she expected.

Way more.

\\\\\\\\\\\\\\\\\\\\\\\\\\\\\\\\\\\\\\\\\

Rivka nearly tripped over a pair of boots, attached to the girl nestled in the corner.

"Cat!" Rivka gasped, almost dropping Chickpea's dinner.

Cat blinked twice, like she was a cat herself who had just woken up, and pulled her earbuds out of her ears. "What?"

Rivka clutched the grain bucket to her chest, staring in disbelief. "Where have you been?"

Cat tilted her head to one side. "I've been here all afternoon."

"I'm so, so sorry," said Rivka dropping to her knees. "I was awful."

Cat looked away. "Yeah, you were."

Chickpea butted her nose between them, trying to get to the grain.

"I think we'd better let them eat," said Cat, standing up and brushing straw off her pants.

Rivka poured the grain into the bin, and the girls slipped out of the stall. While Rivka got hay and alfalfa for Chickpea, Cat watched the foal nurse.

"Peanut is the perfect name," Cat mused.

"You mean for the foal?"

Cat nodded.

"It's cute. I like it."

"Cool."

"Can I ask you something?"

Cat nodded again.

"Why did you say you hated babies?"

Cat didn't answer for so long that Rivka started to feel anxious all over again. She didn't want people asking her stuff about herself, and here she was doing it to Cat. She was about to apologize again when Cat spoke. "I don't really hate babies. But my mom keeps having them one after another, and with each one she has less time for me. All I get anymore is *Cat, change the baby. Cat, put the baby to bed. Cat, read the baby a story.* She's got nothing left for me."

"That sucks," said Rivka.

Cat let out a big breath. "More than you know."

# CHAPTER FIFTEEN

**C**at was on lockdown for a week.

For sneaking her smartphone out of the desk drawer in the office, she was sentenced to cleaning the chicken coop. For scaring everyone while she was missing, she forfeited free time and got extra chores. Worst of all for someone who liked her space, the Bridles had put her on the buddy system 24/7. Madison was even sleeping in the bunk below her. She rode during lesson time with the rest of them. It was the only time Rivka ever caught a smile on her face, but even that was fleeting.

Every morning Rivka worked with Rowdy. He was exactly what Madison had said—a stubborn one. If she didn't sit the right way and use her legs the right way and hold the reins the right way, he stood there like a rock. But slowly the pieces were coming together. She was figuring it out.

Rivka just wished she could figure out Cat.

They hadn't talked again about the blowup in the arena. Whenever Rivka tried to talk to her, Cat answered in short, clipped sentences.

When she finally earned her free time back, Rivka, Sam, and Lauren set up the net and corn hole board for Cat's crazy, made-up game.

"Wanna play Frattleprat?" Rivka begged.

Cat shrugged and kept reading her comic book.

"Come on," said Rivka, tugging on her arm. "We all want to play, and we need you."

"Yeah, right."

"Two on two," Lauren prodded.

"I can add."

"But can you do the Fibonacci sequence?" Sam asked.

Rivka rolled her eyes. Cat ignored him.

"Look," said Rivka, flopping into the hammock next to Cat. "I apologized! I know I got you in trouble. I'm sorry."

Cat didn't look up. "Doesn't matter."

"I shouldn't have yelled at you."

Cat turned the page in her comic book. "Take-home message," she said, more to herself than anyone else. "Don't try to make nice. There's no freaking point."

"But there is," Rivka protested, on the verge of tears. "I don't want us to be the Antisocials."

Rivka caught a tiny twitch at the corner of Cat's mouth. Desperate to turn that twitch into a proper smile, Rivka grabbed three beanbags in each hand and flung them over the net, yelling at the top of her lungs, "FRATTLEPRAT!!!!"

At that exact moment, Carla and Paul walked around the corner of the house, deep in conversation. A beanbag whizzed toward Paul, and he dodged just in time. Another nearly whacked Carla, but she snatched it out of the air like a professional baseball player. The others thudded to the ground.

Their expressions were so shocked, so utterly surprised, and so completely hilarious that all the kids lost it. Rivka thought she might pee her pants from laughing so hard. Even Paul and Carla cracked up.

"What on earth is Frattleprat?" Carla asked, when she finally caught her breath.

"A net-bounded, target-trajectory game that eschews rackets," said Sam in a clipped monotone.

Carla's mouth fell open.

"I told you," said Paul, trying to keep a straight face, "this is the best group we've ever had. They're like kidbots or something."

Sam did a warped version of the robot dance in their direction. "Do. You. Want. To. Frattle. Prat?"

"Ohmygosh," gasped Carla. "Y'all are hilarious. Come on, Paul," she said, pulling on his arm. "Let's dance or frattle or whatever."

Rivka held out a hand to Cat. "Truce?"

Cat frowned at her, but she took Rivka's hand and squeezed it.

"Will you play?" Rivka pleaded.

"Oh, fine," said Cat, rolling her eyes, and pretty soon, there were beanbags flying everywhere.

\\\\\\\\\\\\\\\\\\\\\\\\\\\\\\\\\\\\\\\\\\\\\

Rivka's good feelings didn't even last through dinner.

There was a knock halfway through the meal, and Mr. Bridle greeted and ushered in a stocky, bow-legged man who looked like he'd spent his whole life on horseback.

He had black hair, dark skin, and a weathered face. Sadness edged the corners of his eyes and mouth.

He took off his cowboy hat and held his hand out to Mr. Bridle.

Mr. Bridle hugged him instead, and Paul rose from the table to do the same.

"Hola, Álvaro," said Paul, bear-hugging the man and whacking his back man-style. "I am so sorry. Can't believe old Gooselegs is being such an a—"

Mr. Bridle cleared his throat loudly, and Paul swallowed the rest of his sentence.

"Shoot," said Paul, releasing Álvaro. "I'm spitting mad."

Álvaro nodded slowly, worrying the brim of his hat in his hands. "It has been a shock."

Paul shook his head in disgust. "He was always a big-headed jerk when we both ranched on the Big R."

"I appreciate your help," Álvaro told him and Mr. Bridle.

Ma Etty joined them and gave Álvaro a peck on the cheek. "You're always welcome here."

He kissed her back. "You have a big heart, Henrietta."

She turned back to the kids at the table. "We're going with Álvaro to pick up his things. I need you kids to help Madison and Fletch with cleanup and then get some sleep. Don't let the bed bugs bite!"

She tried to sound cheery on that last bit, but no one was very convinced. "All right, gentlemen," she said, reaching for Paul and Mr. Bridle. "Let's get this over with."

As soon as Paul, Álvaro, and the Bridles were out the door, Cat said, "What in the heck was that all about? Ma Etty looks like she's going to a funeral."

Fletch and Madison had some sort of silent conversation across the table.

"What?!" Cat demanded.

Fletch let out a big sigh. "There's a lot going on at the ranches around here." He pushed back from the table. "Let's get to these dishes."

Cat crossed her arms over her chest. "No way. Not until you tell us what's up."

More silent glances between the trainers.

Cat let out her breath in a huff. "Fine. We'll just imagine the worst, then."

Rivka looked up from her hands. How did Cat know that that was exactly what she was doing?

Finally Madison caved. "Álvaro is—was—a ranch hand on a big ranch farther down the Colorado River. He's a dang good cowboy. But the foreman is this guy that everybody calls Gooselegs."

"Real name is Herman Graves," added Fletch.

"He's descended from one of the first pioneer families in the area. Fell on hard times a few years ago. Lost the family ranch, and now he's bitter as heck about having to work someone else's land. Blames the Mexicans for everything."

"Álvaro isn't even Mexican," said Madison. "He's originally from Peru."

Fletch nodded.

"Did they try to beat him up too?" Rivka asked in a small voice.

Madison shook her head. "Gooselegs fired him. Apparently he said something like, 'From now on, only Americans work for me.' "

Fletch's expression turned stony. " 'Course, what he meant was 'white people.'"

Rivka heard the hurt and the anger in his voice, and underneath that, a hint of fear.

And she knew exactly what that felt like—the sick feeling in the pit of her stomach, the way she'd looked differently at people on the street, wondering if that man or that woman was the one who'd painted the swastika.

This was why she couldn't be Jewish anymore.

This was why she couldn't go through with the bat mitzvah.

It was just too scary.

The riled-up voices of Madison, Fletch, and the other kids tumbled through her: "Poor Álvaro" . . . "Not fair" . . . "That's horrible" . . . "What about his family?" Rivka dug her fingernails into the palms of her hands under the table. She had to get out of here, right now. Before she completely lost it. The second that Fletch herded the other kids toward cleanup duties, Rivka took Madison aside.

"I don't feel good," she said. "I need to go lie down."

Madison felt her forehead. "I don't think you have a fever."

"My stomach hurts."

"Do you want some Tums or something?"

"I want to lie down."

Madison nodded. "Okay. Off to bed with you. You'll owe these guys on dish duty, though."

"Got it."

Sam was already complaining when Rivka slipped out the front door, but she let Madison deal with the blowback.

The horses were still in the pasture. Rowdy, as usual, had his nose in the tallest clump of grass he could find. She helped him reach the tastiest bits, and he nuzzled her shoulder while he chewed. Rivka scratched the whorl under his forelock. Why couldn't everything be as simple as a pony eating grass and getting his itchy spots taken care of?

*Stubborn, stubborn, stubborn.*

That's what her parents said about her refusal to return to the synagogue for any reason. Rivka had no idea how to make them understand. Rowdy was stubborn too. She liked that about him. It forced her to work hard. She had to sit right, ask right, encourage right, to get him to respond. Madison said that made him feel safe, because Rowdy knew that she wouldn't take him someplace he shouldn't be or ask him to do something dangerous.

She heard voices from the kitchen. Everyone inside was finishing up. Rivka didn't want to be caught shirking on chores. She didn't want to have to explain how being with Rowdy calmed her down. And she definitely didn't want to talk to anyone. She gave him one more scratch and a kiss on the nose and ran to the bunkhouse.

By the time the others came in, she was in her bunk pretending to sleep.

## CHAPTER SIXTEEN

"**O**kay, everyone," Ma Etty announced after breakfast a week later. "This is the big moment. Cat, will you do the honors?" The old woman held an old coffee can full of slips of paper.

"Me?" Cat looked surprised.

It had been a weird week. Rivka had kept to herself. Cat had been sulking around the cabin reading comics. Sam had picked up a new obsession, bird-watching, which meant that all he ever did was crane his neck up to the sky with a pair of binoculars stuck to his eyeballs. And Lauren was just Lauren.

Ma Etty smiled at Cat. "Yes, you." She held out the can and shook it.

They had settled on three top choices for the

foal's name: Biscuit, Peanut, and Nugget. Everyone who came to the ranch got to vote. Rivka had been lobbying hard for Peanut, which had been Cat's suggestion. It seemed like the least she could do after what had happened.

Cat took the can.

"I'll tally for you," Sam offered, grabbing a notebook and pencil off the counter. In big block letters, he wrote the three names, and as Cat pulled each slip out and read it, he made a hash mark under the appropriate column.

In the last week, there had been several late-night meetings with ranch hands from the surrounding areas about mounting a protest at the upcoming anti-immigrant rally. Rivka didn't like overhearing the meetings. She didn't like the raised voices that came from the big house or the way fear clung to visitors.

But Ma Etty had asked Rivka and the rest to help out with the little children who came. Usually they taught them to play Frattleprat until the shrieking and laughter got them banished to the barn, and then they let the kids give treats to the horses. One night they'd gotten them to vote on a name for the baby. Translated into Spanish, the names were Galleta, Maní, Pepita. Odds were high on Maní—Peanut.

The Spanish-speaking voters hadn't been keen on giving the little colt a name that was a feminine noun.

Sam and Cat got to work tallying up all the votes. Rivka bounced in the chair next to Cat, peering over her shoulder.

"While you're all gathered here," said Mr. Bridle, "we've got a bit of an announcement."

Cat and Sam paused. Rivka noticed the worried look on her friend's face and hoped no one was in trouble, but then she saw Paul's huge grin and relaxed.

"Ma Etty and I have checked in with your trainers." He gave a nod to Fletch and Madison. "And we understand that you are all making great progress in the saddle."

"Definitely!" Madison chimed in.

"And you haven't been giving them any trouble."

Fletch agreed. "Unless you count making us all memorize the birds-of-Colorado list."

Everyone laughed, including Sam, but he didn't look up from his work. Mr. Bridle patted him on the shoulder.

"Paul has offered to take you all on a pack trip," the old man continued.

"What's that?" Lauren asked.

"Only the best thing ever!" Madison said. "We take the horses and head into the mountains and camp out."

Lauren looked dubious. "Like on the ground?"

"Exactly!" Paul crowed. "Fishing, campfires, and fun. What more could any kid want?"

"Disney World?" said Cat, flattening another strip of paper.

Paul pretended that she had stabbed him through the heart. "Just you wait, Cat. It's going to be a blast."

Rivka had never been camping. Her dad was a fan of hotels with crisp sheets and daily housekeeping. A pack trip—she rolled the unfamiliar words around in her head. It sounded like an adventure, and that seemed like a great idea.

"Well," said Ma Etty, turning to Cat and Sam, "do we have a winner?"

"Yes, ma'am," Cat said, taking the sheet of notebook paper from Sam and holding it up. She grinned at Rivka and gave a little fist pump.

The people had spoken.

The foal's name was Peanut!

\\\\\\\\\\\\\\\\\\\\\\\\\\\\\\\\\\\\\\\\\\\\\\

Planning for the pack trip was a huge undertaking. Each day, before free time, the kids planned and prepared. They had lists of camping equipment, horse gear, and personal items. They'd written menus and made shopping lists. They'd scoured the map of the surrounding national forest land and laid out their route.

Tomorrow they were off!

Rivka couldn't wait.

The mound of gear they were assembling seemed massive to Rivka. Carla had helped them pull together two first-aid kits—one for the humans and one for the horses. Paul had found saddlebags for each kid's horse. They would also have three pack horses, which would carry what he called panniers. They looked like two duffel bags connected by straps that went over the horse's back.

"Personal gear in the saddlebags. Sleeping bag tied behind the saddle. Everything else we take has got to fit in these babies," said the ranch manager, indicating the panniers. "No nonessentials."

"Like your harmonica?" Cat teased.

"That's essential!"

"What if there's no room?"

"I will leave behind my toothbrush," Paul said in a serious voice.

Fletch came up behind them and made a face. "I'm not sharing a tent with you."

Paul pretended to cry.

"Poor, sad panda," said Madison, patting him on the shoulder.

Mr. Bridle chuckled. "This crew might not make it past Fool's Butte."

"I'll take that as a challenge," said Paul and began hustling the kids into action. "Sam and Lauren, I want you guys to come to the grocery store with me to pick up the last of the fresh food. Cat and Rivka, you're in charge of packing the dry food and cook kit. Ma Etty can help you."

The girls saluted and headed to the big house.

"Down here," said Ma Etty, leading them into the basement. Shelves lined the concrete walls. Some held jars of peaches and strawberry jam. There were rows of pickles—cucumber, asparagus, and dilly beans—and brightly colored chutneys. At the far end were trays of mismatched silverware, various sizes of dented pots, and stacks of metal plates and cups.

"You'll need seven sets," she said. "One for each of you kids and also Madison, Fletch, and Paul. I'm sure sad that Mr. Bridle and I aren't coming along."

"Someone has to keep an eye on Chickpea and Peanut," said Rivka.

Ma Etty nodded. "That's true."

Cat picked up one of the plates and examined it. The white enamel finish covering the metal plate was faintly scratched with silvery tine marks. In several places, the black enamel stripe around the rim had chipped off, and the tinge of rusted metal was visible. "These look like they are about a hundred years old," said Cat.

"Could be older," said Ma Etty. "Mr. Bridle's family has been here for a long time. Back in the old days, that was fine dinnerware."

"Were they pioneers?" Rivka asked. "Did they come here in covered wagons?" She'd always been fascinated by Lewis and Clark and the Oregon Trail. She wondered what it would have been like to travel so far and know that you'd probably never see your family back home ever again.

"Mr. Bridle's great-grandpa was one of the early settlers here in Quartz Creek. But his grandmother was the one who really knew the land. She was Paiute, one of a long line of leaders in their tribe."

"That's cool," said Cat.

Ma Etty nodded in agreement. "Mr. Bridle

is one quarter Paiute, and one hundred percent Colorado dirt. Don't worry 'bout the math." She helped them select the pots and pans they would need, and they carried everything upstairs to the kitchen. "Better give these dishes a quick wash. The basement is super dusty."

Cat filled one side of the sink with warm, sudsy water, and Rivka prepped the other side of the sink for rinsing. As Ma Etty sorted through ranch mail at the table, she hummed to herself, something a little folksy, a little country. Rivka had never liked that kind of music before, but here on the ranch it seemed like the perfect soundtrack to the clouds and the green and the chickens and the horses. She hoped that Paul would take both his toothbrush and his harmonica.

# CHAPTER SEVENTEEN

**R**ivka was in the barn before anyone else got up. By the time Fletch came in, she had taken care of breakfast for all the horses.

"Look at you," said Fletch, pushing back his cowboy hat. "Thanks for feeding everyone."

"Sure! I'm excited to get going."

He scratched Sawbones between the ears. "Me too. I love a good, long ride. How 'bout we give the horses that we're taking an extra flake of alfalfa, and then go grab breakfast for us?"

Rivka did as he asked and snuck a few pumpkin treats to Rowdy and Chickpea. Little Peanut was bounding around the double-size stall, poking his mother with his nose while she tried to eat. If a horse could look exasperated, Chickpea sure did.

Back at the house, Madison and Álvaro, who had been staying at the ranch, were already at the table digging into a stack of pancakes.

"Do you seriously think you can eat all of that?" Cat asked Madison.

Madison gave her belly an exaggerated rub. "I'm carbo-loading for our trip."

"Me too," said Sam, slathering butter on his pancakes.

Ma Etty was still at the griddle. "How many more do I need to make?"

"Lots," said Paul, slipping off his boots by the front door. "I'm not sure I can manage an entire week without your banana pancakes."

She chuckled and poured batter in neat circles on the sizzling pan. "I sure wish I was coming with all of you."

Rivka filled her plate and sat next to Madison.

"All ready for our ride?" the trainer asked.

Rivka stole a glance at Álvaro, remembering the trouble in town, and the tightness in her stomach returned. "More than you know," she said.

"It'll be awesome," Madison agreed. "I love getting into the backcountry."

Rivka looked down at her plate. "Getting away will be good."

\\\\\\\\\\\\\\\\\\\\\\\\\\\\\\\\\\\\\\\\\\

They set off in a long line, with Fletch in the lead. Cat insisted on being next with Bucky. "I'm the oldest," she announced, as if that were a good justification.

Rivka wondered if it had more to do with a certain good-looking cowboy, but she was wise enough not to mention it as she rode behind Cat. She and Rowdy were next, followed by Sam, Lauren, and Madison, who led one of the pack horses. Paul brought up the rear with the other two.

The horses seemed as eager as the kids.

Rowdy was happy to point his nose toward the mountains and follow along. Madison had explained how it was easier to ride horses like this. They followed each other instead of needing constant guidance from their riders. Not that the riders were allowed to slack off or anything. Madison had been super serious about that.

Rivka made sure her posture was correct and that she was keeping the right tension on the reins, and then she let herself slide into the rhythm of Rowdy's walk. For a long while, the trail followed the creek, and they were shaded by the tall cottonwoods. The horses' hooves beat out a steady rhythm on the dirt trail, and the stream burbled and sang. The sun climbed overhead, and Rivka swayed sleepily in the rising heat.

Occasionally, Fletch pointed out a landmark—Fool's Butte off to their right, a mountain pass used by the pioneers to the left, and the spot where Mr. Bridle had once caught two men trying to steal some of their cattle. Other than that, they rode mostly in silence. Sam had borrowed a pair of binoculars and a bird identification guidebook from Mr. Bridle, which he had tucked in the front pocket of his flannel shirt. "I think that's a hairy woodpecker. Or maybe it's a downy one," he said, fumbling his reins while he tried to look in the guidebook.

"Downy," said Madison. "They're smaller."

Sam ignored her and kept flipping pages.

"You can't just put your horse on autopilot, Sam," she said, when his horse stopped altogether and caused a pileup.

Rivka looked back to see what was going on, and Rowdy took that opportunity to sidestep toward a particularly tasty clump of grass. "Don't let him do that," Madison called, and Rivka pulled on the reins and nudged Rowdy back into a walk.

"None of that," Rivka said to the pony, and he huffed at her. "We've got a long way to go."

\\\\\\\\\\\\\\\\\\\\\\\\\\\\\\\\\\\\\\\\\\\\\

By midday, Rivka's stomach was rumbling, and she was sore from the saddle. She hoped they would be stopping soon. The trail, which rose steadily away from the creek, had narrowed, and the horses plodded along single file. The smell of pine tickled her nose, and she had to pay attention so she didn't get whacked in the face by low-hanging branches.

Up ahead, Fletch's horse navigated a rocky section of trail and then disappeared over a ridge of rock. Rivka forgot her hunger. It was as if he had flown off the edge of the world. A moment later, Cat did the same, and then it was Rowdy carrying her out of the trees and straight into the sky.

Blue as far as Rivka could see—it felt like flying.

The trail had taken them up and over the shoulder of the mountain. On this side, the land sloped down toward a much larger river that twisted and turned far below. Rivka could make out the frothy sections of churning whitewater, but it was too far away to hear the rushing current.

The trees were sparser here. The broad meadow stretching before her was splatter-painted with orange and purple and red wildflowers. Little brown birds—chipping sparrows, according to Sam—hopped and zoomed above the waving grass. The breeze dried the sweat from her face.

"Lunchtime," Fletch announced, dismounting.

Madison did the same, groaning. "I thought you'd never stop!"

The trainers held the horses for Rivka and the other kids so they could clamber down and stretch their stiff legs. The rest of them looked as tired as Rivka felt.

"My butt hurts," said Cat.

"You've got to shake it out," said Paul, doing a wacky, booty-shaking jitterbug.

Everyone burst out laughing.

"Dance party," said Madison, joining in but with a tad more grace.

Still two-stepping, she helped Paul tie the pack horses in the shade where they could nibble on flowers.

"Are we camping here?" Sam asked.

Fletch shook his head. "We'll stay by the river," he said, pointing to the silver squiggle below them.

Sam squinted against the bright sun. "That looks like miles away."

The cowboy shrugged. "Eat now. Complain later."

Rivka unbuckled one of her saddlebags, retrieved her water bottle, and made sure that Rowdy was near plenty of tasty-looking grass before flopping down next to Cat.

Fletch retrieved the bag that held lunch for their first day and began handing out sandwiches, only a little squashed from a morning in saddlebags. Ravenous, they devoured their lunches and washed the dust out of their throats with long swigs of well water. Rivka swirled the contents of her one-liter bottle. It was only about a quarter full. They'd need to refill from the river soon. She peered into the river valley below. Sam was right. It seemed a long way off.

"Can I see your binoculars?" she asked Sam as he pored over his bird guidebook. He unlooped them from his neck and passed them to her with a grunt. She adjusted the eye cups to fit her face and then fingered the focus knob until her view of the river below was clear. In the smooth parts, it was a deep blackish green. The rapids were white and frothy, with a hint of pale green.

Rivka moved her head slowly to the left so she could scan the river upstream. "Are there any swimming holes?"

Madison, who was sitting next to her, said, "I don't know. I haven't been down this way before, but it would be awesome to rinse off this trail dust." She tugged on her long ponytail. "I think I've got dirt between my teeth."

Through the binoculars, Rivka could make out a thin trail threading alongside the rushing water. In a section where the river widened she could see what looked like a pebbly beach on the closer shore. At the very least they could wade. She wiggled her sweaty toes inside her cowboy boots. That would be awesome.

She scanned a little farther upstream to a tumble of boulders and flood-swept logs and branches. It looked like there would be lots of cool places to explore. On the opposite side of the river, she caught sight of a pile of wood that seemed strangely regular. She examined it more closely. The logs were too evenly shaped to be natural. "Hey," she said, tapping Paul on his shoulder. "What's that?"

The cowboy took the binoculars. It took a minute for Rivka to explain where to look, but once he'd found the landmarks she indicated, Paul said, "It looks like an old homestead. Lots of places like that scattered in these mountains. Mr. Bridle knows a ton about them. He's the history buff around here."

He handed the binoculars back, and Rivka looked at the ruined cabin again. She thought of her city—her loud, rushing, brightly colored city. There were people everywhere. The pianist who lived upstairs. The woman next door with an African gray parrot named Chuck. The sidewalks that were never empty. The restaurants that bustled all night. No matter how late it was, if she woke in the night she could hear horns and sirens and the never-ending sounds of traffic.

They'd ridden for over three hours to get this far and the homestead was still a long way away. She couldn't imagine living way out here in the middle of nowhere.

"Can I have those back?" Sam asked.

Rivka lowered the binoculars. He was holding out one hand, eyes glued on a brown bird with a fat bill perched at the top of a nearby tree. She handed them over and began to pack up her lunch things.

After observing and consulting his book, Sam declared it was a female blue grosbeak.

Lauren argued for some kind of sparrow and swiped the guidebook out of his hands.

The two of them argued about it until the brown bird was joined by a bright blue bird with an equally large bill.

"Ha!" Sam crowed. "I told you so. Blue grosbeak. The male proves it."

Lauren stuck her tongue out at him. "Fine. You win."

The descent into the valley was exhilarating. The grass rippled in the wind like waves, and even the horses seemed to perk up as the river rose to meet them. This would be Rivka's first night camping out.

She couldn't wait!

## CHAPTER EIGHTEEN

They set up camp near the river in a grove of trees with silvery-greenish bark and heart-shaped leaves that rustled like tissue paper in the breeze. Paul called them aspens. In an open patch of grass along the shore, there was already a fire pit made of river rocks. Sam, Fletch, and Madison took a handsaw and went off to find some dry, dead limbs for firewood. Paul put the girls to work unpacking the panniers and setting up camp.

"It's going to be a gorgeous night," he crowed, stretching his arms wide to take in the cloudless sky. "Let's sleep under the stars."

"Can we do that?" asked Rivka. "Just sleep out in the big wild everything?"

"Of course," Paul laughed.

"What about ants," said Lauren, "and mosquitos?"

"Snakes?" added Cat. "Wolves?"

The three girls circled the camp, looking up at trees and around rocks.

Paul piled the cook kit and bags of food near the fire pit. "Have any of you been camping before?"

Rivka shook her head. "I went to summer camp, but there were cabins."

"My grandparents took me in their RV," Cat offered.

Lauren drooped against a nearby rock. "This is the first time I've even been away from home."

"I'll give you the lowdown," he said, lining the girls up so they could pass the gear from person to person as he unloaded more panniers. "Too late in the season for mosquitos. Ants are no problem as long as you don't sleep on an ant hill."

"Duh," said Cat.

Paul tipped his hat to her. "Well, Ms. Smarty Pants, yours truly here once put his bedroll smack on a regular mountain of red ants. It was dark. That's my excuse, but in the morning when those little suckers woke up . . . Yee-howdy! That was terrible."

"Okay. Got it," said Cat, trying not to laugh. "No ant hills."

"As for snakes," Paul continued to add to their list of freaky nature stuff. "Gopher snakes, bull snakes . . . you might see some of them, but they're not venomous. Rattlers are mainly in the rocks. And they announce their presence like gentlemen."

"Gentlemen?" Rivka looked dubious.

"What about the wolves?" asked Lauren in a tiny voice.

Paul's face fell. "The last Colorado wolves were shot out of these mountains in the thirties. Sad story."

While they talked, they unloaded the water filter, tarp, rope, camp stove, fuel bottles, sleeping pads, tents, and everything else. By the time their gear was stacked in neat piles near the fire pit, Madison, Sam, and Fletch were back with armloads of wood. Rivka untacked Rowdy and gave him a good brush-down. He was sweaty where the saddle had been and apparently itchy, since as soon as he drank his fill from the river, he found a tree to scratch against, twisting his body this way and that to get all the spots.

Fletch helped Paul rig what they called a high line so that the horses could be tethered safely and still have plenty of access to grass. Rowdy seemed perfectly content with this solution. When Rivka saw him with a bouquet of wildflowers hanging out of his mouth, she made sure that Madison took a picture with the camera Ma Etty had sent along.

"Last thing to do," said Paul, "is figure out the sleeping arrangements. I'm going to put a ground cloth over there and put my sleeping bag on it and call it good. If any of you are still worried about ants and ghost wolves and the like . . ." He gave the girls a pointed look. "Then you should put up a tent." Lauren insisted on putting up a tent and Sam helped her, but everyone else decided to sleep out.

"Now commences my favorite part of camping," Madison announced when all the chores were done.

"I'm afraid to ask," said Fletch, shaking his head.

"The napping part!" She unfurled a nylon back-packing hammock and hung it between two trees. "Wake me up when dinner's ready," she called, settling in with a sigh.

"I thought you were the cook tonight," he teased.

She plugged him with finger guns. "You're it."

To the kids he said, "Free time. Until we cook dinner for the queen. If you are going to explore around camp, you need to take a partner. Ma Etty insists on the buddy system out here."

The reminder made Cat flinch, but she didn't argue.

Fletch settled himself against a rock in the sun to read. Lauren and Sam took off downstream to go bird-watching. Paul pulled out a plastic cylinder about the length of Rivka's arm, unscrewed the top, and pulled out a fishing rod in four parts. As she and Cat watched, he assembled the rod and threaded the line through a series of small metal loops down its length.

"Have either of you done any fly fishing?" he asked, holding the end of the line in one corner of his mouth.

"Nope," said Rivka. "Nobody in my family fishes."

Cat shook her head. "I've gone out spin casting a few times, but never fly fishing. Can I try?"

"Absolutely." Paul put on a fishing vest and pulled a small box out of one pocket. Inside were rows of imitation flies tied on hooks. "How about this one?" he asked, pointing to a tiny brown fly with flecks of gold in its fluffy middle.

Cat shrugged. "Looks buggy to me."

Paul tied on the fly and gestured for them to follow him upstream. About a half mile from camp,

Paul stopped. "This is good water. See the way there's a patch of calm behind those big submerged rocks? There's probably a big, fat trout down there hanging out and eating caddis."

"What's a caddis?" Rivka asked.

Paul's face lit up. "Check this out." He propped the fly rod against a tree, knelt at the river's edge, and reached into the cold water. He picked a smooth, palm-sized rock and flipped it over. Rivka and Cat leaned in close to see what he was pointing at. They looked like inch-long sticks . . . until they started moving!

"Whaaaat?" Cat said, drawing out the question.

The sticks were really small tubes. Inside each one was some kind of insect that poked its head and legs out of the opening and crawled over the wet surface of the rock, dragging its little tube house.

"Caddis fly larvae," Paul explained, picking one up. "They make these casings out of rock and sand. Pretty awesome."

"Pretty weird," said Rivka. Bugs weren't her most favorite thing in the world.

Cat held out her hand, and Paul dropped the caddis into her palm. "It tickles," she said, watching it crawl around.

"There's this artist who makes jewelry out of the cases," said Paul.

Rivka quirked an eyebrow at him. "Who wears bug jewelry?"

"She raises them in an aquarium. Instead of regular old rock or sand, she gives them tiny chunks of semiprecious stones like amethyst or turquoise."

"And they make the cases fancy?"

"You got it."

"Whoa," said Cat. "I'd like to see those."

Paul grinned at her. "Next time we go to town I can show you the gallery that sells her jewelry."

"That'd be cool."

Rivka made a face. "I'm not sure I want to wear bug parts as earrings."

"Suit yourself," Paul said with a chuckle. "Okay, gals, let's set you up to catch us some dinner."

# CHAPTER NINETEEN

**C**at turned out to be a natural with a fly rod. But every time Rivka tried to loop the line overhead and launch the fly into parts of the river that Paul said looked "trouty," all she managed to do was catch the hook in a tree or tie the line in a knot. Finally, she gave up and decided to explore upstream.

"Don't go too far," Paul called. "Stay in earshot."

She gave him the thumbs-up and began to poke slowly along the shore. Her shuffling footsteps scared a frog out of the long grass. It went soaring into the river with a *kerplop*, just like that grade-school song about the banks of the Hanky-Pank. She hummed to herself as she walked. Around the next bend, the river widened. She could see the pebbled bottom all the way across, and on the other side was the ruin she'd seen from the ridgetop.

It was larger than she'd realized. The logs were as big around as her waist. She wondered how the pioneers had transported them. They must have used horses or oxen to drag them into place. Would Rowdy do that for her? Could he be a pioneer pony? The front wall was still mostly standing. The opening where the door had been was crooked and sunken, but she could imagine the cabin when it was new—a stout, square structure built to last.

Rivka sat down on the grass, trying to imagine living here. Right now it was sunny and warm and apparently "trouty." What about winter? She knew it snowed a lot in Colorado. Maybe it would drift higher and higher until snow skimmed the edges of the now-collapsed roof. There would be wood to chop and water to haul and a million things to do to survive.

It was hard to imagine no Chinese takeout, no ice-skating rink with tinny music over the speakers, no escaping dreary afternoons in the movie theater down the street from her brownstone apartment. What Rivka's father announced on a regular basis was true—they were city people. Every single one of Rivka's aunts and uncles and cousins and second cousins lived in the city—Providence or Baltimore or New York. *Avoid the wilderness* was practically a family motto. The old people didn't even like to have picnics.

And here she was, flying in the face of convention. She had peed outside. She had set up camp. And while she might not have held the caddis like Cat did, she had poked it with her finger. That seemed like accomplishment enough. Tonight she was going to sleep out under the stars. Her aunts would never believe it.

"Skunked," said Cat, coming up the trail toward her. Rivka looked over her shoulder and sniffed. Cat giggled. "If you smell anything bad, it's Paul, not me."

"Hey!" he protested. To Rivka, he said, "What have you been up to?"

She pointed across the river at the abandoned cabin. "Can we wade over there and explore?"

Paul pushed his cowboy hat back and checked out the river. "Don't know why not. Let's do it." He leaned the fly rod against a tree and sat down to pull off his boots. "We should probably take our shoes with us." He unloaded his day pack and left the contents by the fly rod. "Pop your boots in here."

Rivka rolled up her pant legs and tested the water. "It's really cold."

"Snow melt," said Paul, pointing to the still white-topped mountains.

He held out his hands to the girls, and they linked together for the crossing. Rivka felt along the bottom with her toes. The rocks were smooth and a tiny bit slimy underfoot. She tried not to think of caddis fly nymphs or whatever else could be down there. The rushing water tugged at her legs, but it never got above knee-high. Even so, her toes were numb by the time they reached the other side, and she had to rub the blood back into them.

Once she had her boots back on, Rivka walked around the outside of the cabin, running her fingers along the weathered wood. She was so curious about who had lived here. Maybe a gold miner or a rancher? She wondered if there had been kids with cornhusk dolls, like she learned about in school. Had Mr. Bridle's great-grandfather known them?

Back at the front of the cabin, she stepped gingerly inside. There was no floor, just the pile of fallen-in roof boards. Grass, wildflowers, and young trees grew up through the decaying wreck of the cabin. In the far corner was a broken jumble of old canning jars. The rusting remains of a potbellied wood stove stood in the other corner. She stepped inside and turned in a circle, trying to imagine living inside these four walls. When Rivka had completed a full revolution and was facing the opening again, a black mark above the door caught her eye.

It was seared into the fading wood.

The shape looked like a capital R, except the long part of the R extended downward and hooked into a J.

"Check this out," she called to Paul and Cat, who joined her inside. "What do you think that means?"

Paul reached up and ran a finger along the shape. "That. Is. Amazing."

"I don't get it," said Cat. "Pioneer graffiti?"

Rivka's heart flip-flopped. *Graffiti.* "Does it mean something bad?"

Paul tugged on his mustache. "It's a cattle brand, and yours truly happens to know exactly whose it is. Or rather, was."

"You do?" Cat looked at him like he had just solved a big mystery case.

Paul explained. "Mr. Bridle is really into history,

and recently he showed me a list of brands he had dug up, all the marks for the earliest ranch families in the state. This is one of them."

"Do you have a photographic memory or something?" Rivka asked, thinking about how she had struggled to keep the letters of the Hebrew alphabet from getting all mixed up in her brain.

"No way," said Paul, "but I remember this one because it stands for Rachel Jacobs. See, R and J put together."

"Wow. She must have been super tough, living way out here," said Cat.

"It gets better. Rachel was one of three sisters, each with their own brand. Bella Jacobs ranched in Nevada, and Hannah ran cattle in California. On top of that . . ." he said, turning to Rivka, "they were Jewish. Mr. Bridle has a whole book back at the ranch about pioneer Jews in the Old West."

Rivka could hardly believe it. Jewish pioneers on the Oregon Trail. Why hadn't she ever learned that bit of history?

". . . but I remembered the RJ brand," Paul was saying, "because apparently Ms. Jacobs lived out here all by herself. Lots of people tried to get her to move to town. Her dad tried to marry her off, but she told him in no uncertain terms that all she needed was a good horse." He chuckled.

"She sounds stubborn," said Cat. There was an edge to her voice that caught Rivka's attention. *Stubborn.*

"Sounds like Ma Etty," said Paul, unaware of how Cat's expression had hardened.

But Rivka noticed. And even though Cat had turned away, Rivka heard her mutter, "Stubborn girls," more to herself than anyone else. "Parents hate that."

## CHAPTER TWENTY

**B**y the time they got back to camp, Fletch had a fire going in the fire pit, and Sam had started laying out plates and cups for dinner. A mesh bag full of fresh corn, still in the husk, was soaking in the river. Fletch had cut and sharpened green sticks for roasting hot dogs. Lauren was laying out buns, only a little squashed from the panniers, and condiments. Fletch retrieved the corn and tucked each ear into a thick layer of coals. He put Rivka in charge of turning them every few minutes until they were tender. Pretty soon, everyone was crouching around the fire holding skewered hot dogs over the flames.

Rivka's stomach rumbled.

Madison grinned at her. "Hungry much?"

Paul's stick dipped a little too close to the coals and a row of black blisters rose on his hot dog. He pulled it out for inspection.

"Amateur move, dude," Madison teased.

He assumed a stiff-backed, stiff-upper-lip pose. "You know nothing of food, young lady. All the finest chefs recommend blackened salmon and blackened chicken and—"

"Blackened hot dog?" Madison snarked.

"Exactly." Paul raised a pinky finger and slid the charred hot dog onto a bun. He made a big show of eating it with delicate gusto, and everyone laughed.

After they were done eating, Fletch put more wood on the fire, and Paul played the harmonica while Madison forced everyone to sing "She'll Be Coming 'Round the Mountain" and "Little Bunny Foo Foo." *There is no escaping camp songs*, Rivka thought, as they roared into the final verse. Jewish camp, horse camp—they all did camp songs. When Madison had exhausted her musical repertoire, she brought out marshmallows, graham crackers, and milk chocolate bars.

"Let's get roasting!"

"Hey, Paul," said Fletch as he skewered two

marshmallows on his roasting stick, "how about one of your famous ghost stories?"

"Don't want to scare the wee ones," Paul said, passing the bag of marshmallows to Rivka.

Cat snorted. "We don't scare easy." Lauren shifted uneasily next to her, and Cat gave Lauren the side-eye before adding, "Well, not all of us."

"I want a ghost story," said Rivka. "A scary one."

Paul stroked his mustache and gazed into the fire. The flames flickered red and orange, casting shadows on his craggy, suddenly serious face. "You know," he said in a low, gravelly voice, "there are many who walk unseen in the darkness of these hills." He paused, and the kids drew closer. Suddenly the night around them felt thick with shadows. "I will tell you the story of the Gray Lady if you think you're brave enough to hear it."

Rivka shuddered, and across the fire, Lauren's eyes grew big and round.

"She was not always the Gray Lady. Once, a long time ago, she was a girl like you." Paul looked from Rivka to Lauren to Cat and back to Rivka. "A girl who dreamed of wide open spaces."

Rivka thought of the buildings back home, how their height cut off the sky and squeezed against the streets.

"But this girl had never left the town where she was born. She grew up and taught in the school, and the children loved her. And every day when the schoolhouse emptied, she walked home to the house she grew up in and made dinner for her mother and father."

Sam's marshmallow went up in a burst of blue-green flames. "I'm not scared yet," he said.

"Ah," said Paul, "a skeptic."

Sam frowned at him and popped the blackened marshmallow into his mouth. "I'm just saying your story is kinda boring."

Paul held up his hands, shushing Sam. "Just you wait."

Sam sniffed at him.

"One day, a wagon train came through town. These families were heading for Oregon, and the girl who was now a teacher went with them. She rode a gray horse the color of storm clouds. The trail was long and hard. She rode for hours every day, and even though she was bone-weary and her body ached, she told stories to the children around the campfire at night, and they loved her."

Sam cleared his throat very loudly, and Madison threw a marshmallow at him.

Paul cleared his throat even more loudly and continued. "The trouble began once they passed Courthouse Rock. The first to die was a boy, one of the teacher's favorites, who was run over by a wagon. That night she could hardly speak for the tears, but the children wanted a story, and she told them one.

"A few days later, an entire family took sick with cholera, and they were buried all in a row—one, two, three, four, five, six. There were fewer faces around the fire that night, and the teacher's heart ached. A week later another wagon was gone, swept away trying to cross the Platte River.

"The living were grief-stricken. They walked the trail in a daze. That night the teacher turned away from the fire and the faces of the remaining children. She did not have the strength to face them. But then . . ."

Paul gazed into the flames for a long moment. Rivka and the others leaned forward, hanging on his words.

"But then she heard them. Faint sounds over the crackle of the fire. A rustling like dried leaves. A high-pitched, mournful call. The far-off gabble of voices."

Paul shifted his position, cocked his head to one side, and listened.

Rivka couldn't help listening too. Her ears reached out into the darkness. The glowing coals popped and hissed. From behind her came the huffing breath of a horse on the high line. A hoof stomp.

And something else . . .

She strained to make it out.

A whispering breath, a far-off warble.

Around the fire pit, no one moved. It seemed they hardly even breathed. Even Sam was frozen in place. One of the horses let out a loud snort, and Rivka jumped.

Paul continued. "The teacher turned back to the fire and told another story. But there was no end to the trouble. The oxen succumbed to drought. The horses died from starvation and snake bite. Even the teacher's gray horse, the one that looked like a storm brewing, gave up before they'd crossed Wyoming.

"Word of their tragedies spread up and down the trail. People said the wagon train was cursed. A boy was hit by lightning. Another, trampled by bison. One by one, the number of people dwindled. Without her horse, the teacher was forced to walk, and her feet blistered and bled. Dust coated her throat until she thought she would choke on it. But every night the teacher told a story. And every night children gathered to listen in a rustling, shifting crowd.

"At Fort Hall, a woman urged her to leave the trail. 'There are so few of you left,' she said. 'We need a teacher here,' she begged. 'Stay.'

"'But the children,' the teacher protested. 'I cannot leave them.' The woman looked at what was left of the group that had left Missouri. Two wagons drawn by emaciated oxen. An old man and a young man and the teacher."

Paul's face glowed in the firelight. He looked at each of them in turn. In the still moment, Rivka again heard what sounded like voices off in the distance.

Paul went on. "But the teacher continued on the trail. The old man died, and the young man died, and each day the teacher walked on alone, leading the last of the oxen. Each night, she stoked the fire and told stories to the children—or at least the ghosts of the children." Paul's voice dropped even lower. "They say the Gray Lady still walks the trail, and if you meet her and if you're brave enough to ask, she will tell you a story."

A burst of sparks flew from the fire, and sound exploded around them. Rivka's stomach lurched.

She clung to Cat as the whispering voices grew into a caterwauling of screaming laughter and eerie yowls. Lauren shrieked and nearly jumped into Fletch's lap.

"What in the heck?" said Sam, jumping up and peering into the darkness.

Paul reached for Sam, pulling him back down. He patted Rivka's shoulder. "Calm down, everyone. Those are coyotes. When they really get going, they sound more like ghosts than anything."

Still jittery, Rivka and the others settled back into their spots around the fire, and for a long time, they all listened to the otherworldly chorus of yips and barks and howls until the sounds of the pack faded off into the distance.

# CHAPTER TWENTY-ONE

**N**o ghosts came in the night. No coyotes either. About the only scary thing was Paul's snoring, which was loud enough to raise a corpse. The first time Rivka woke, she thought it must be the growl of a bear. The second time, she knew it was Paul and couldn't help but giggle. The night was cold and clear. Rivka snuggled deeper into her sleeping bag and lay awake for a while, staring up at the midnight sky. The Milky Way was a swirl of sparkles. It reminded her of a story from Hebrew school about an old rabbi who said that everyone should have two slips of paper, one in each pocket. On one slip of paper it should say *I am but dust and ashes*, and the other should say *The world was created for me*. Sometimes you need to reach into your pocket, the old rabbi had said. The trick is knowing which slip of paper you need to read.

The cold night air skimmed her cheeks. The people around her were good people. And those stars! It really did feel like a world created for her. Rivka fell asleep watching the sky and thinking of Rachel Jacobs living way out here, the absolute ruler of her own universe.

*Not a bad idea*, she thought. *Not a bad idea at all.*

In the morning, she woke curled up in a ball down near Madison's feet and absolutely starving. "What's for breakfast?"

Madison pulled her sleep-wild hair into a ponytail. "What are you fixing?"

"Takeout," said Rivka, thinking of her favorite breakfast spot, the Waffle Window.

"Ha! I think we planned to do bannock with peanut butter and honey."

Rivka zipped her fleece and pulled on her boots. "What's bannock? Is it as good as waffles?"

"Yes," said Fletch with authority. "You will not be disappointed. You'll see."

"Hey," Rivka asked, scanning the campsite, "where's Cat?"

"In the tent," said Lauren. "Still asleep."

"When did she decide to go in there?"

Lauren shrugged. "Said she heard things in the night . . . weird things."

"Better get her up," said Madison. "It's time to get cracking."

After they'd brushed their teeth and spit into the bushes, Rivka helped Fletch relight the campfire. There were still some hot coals from the previous night under a thick layer of ash, and he showed her how to add small twigs and coax the fire to life again. The rest of the crew woke up slowly. Paul was last of all, rubbing sleep from his eyes and moaning about coffee.

"Don't be such a baby," Madison teased as she measured coffee grounds into a percolator. "Your morning fix is on the way."

Sam and Lauren used a handsaw to cut an alder branch into sections that were about two feet long and an inch in diameter. Fletch mixed up a batch of thick, biscuit-like dough and showed the kids how to wrap it around the peeled end of a stick. Pretty soon, they were crouched around the fire, trying not to scorch their meal. When the dough had puffed up and turned golden-brown, Madison helped each of them slide the tube of flaky goodness onto a plate and fill the center with peanut butter and honey.

Fletch was right: Delicious!

That settled it. Rivka was never going home. She didn't need the sideways glances, the not-so-subtle guilt trips, or the shadow of her super-perfect brother. She needed baked dough and honey. That was it.

\\\\\\\\\\\\\\\\\\\\\\\\\\\\\\\\\\\\\\\\\\\\\\\\\\\

Rivka walked to the river's edge to wash the stickiness off her hands. She watched a dragonfly twist and hover near her toe. Everything about the day felt lazy. The current here was slow, and flecks of foam from the faster water upstream curled over the surface of the water. The sun spread across the rocky cliffs on the far side of the river.

She was thinking about the book in her saddle-bag and maybe another visit to the ruined cabin as she walked back to camp.

Paul was getting his fishing things ready.

"Gonna bring us back some trout this time, cow-boy?" Madison asked.

He tucked a granola bar in the front pocket of his flannel shirt. "I will try to bring you a tasty morsel, m'lady."

The trainer gave him a little curtsy. "Fletch and I thought we'd take the crew and ride up to check out that golden eagle's nest on the ridge. Sam is keen to see it."

"Sounds good," said Paul. "Can you manage without me so I can get all zen with my fly rod?"

She waved him off. "Pshaw! We've got this."

After Paul had trekked out of the campsite, Madison started herding everyone else into action. "Time for the great eagle adventure."

Sam had been up since dawn, it seemed. He had already completed five sudoku puzzles and a crossword. Now, he had a baseball cap on backward and binoculars slung around his neck. He tapped a pencil on the edge of his bird notebook. "Come on, people. Time's a-wasting!"

Lauren sidled up next to him. "Can I see your bird list?"

His face brightened. He flipped the notebook open and started to read. "Nighthawk. Did you see them last night? Super cool. Northern flicker. Hairy woodpecker. Scrub jay. Cliff swallow . . ."

Rivka tuned him out.

Cat finally crawled out of the tent and joined her. "Where's Paul?"

"Gone fishing."

Cat's face fell. "What? He's gone already?"

Rivka nodded. "I heard him tell Madison he wouldn't be back until this afternoon."

"Crap."

"You wanted to go?"

"Yeah."

"That's a bummer," said Rivka. "Apparently, we're all going eagle watching."

Cat shot a death glare at Sam. "Great. Just freaking great. I can hardly wait to spend all day on a cliff top watching eagles." She grabbed the bannock Madison had saved for her, slumped back into the tent, flopped on her sleeping bag, and buried her nose in a *Swamp Thing* comic book.

"Mountain chickadee, pygmy nuthatch, song sparrow," Sam droned on.

Rivka looked at her sleeping bag with longing. What about reading? What about being lazy? Hadn't Madison said that was her favorite thing about camping?

But apparently the bird-watching trip up the mountain was not optional. Rivka went to work grooming Rowdy. As she brushed him, she listened to the buzzing, twittering, whirring sounds all around. At least during the daytime, nothing sounded like ghost children.

"Come on, Cat," said Madison, shaking the top of the tent. "You need to saddle up your horse."

Her response came through the zipped door. "Not coming."

"We need to stick together," said Madison, pursing her lips. When she made that face, she reminded Rivka of her mom.

And the arguments.

And her refusals.

"I'm tired and my butt hurts," said Cat. "I hate birds."

Madison unzipped the door of the tent and crouched. Rivka couldn't hear what she was saying, but after a moment, Cat crawled out scowling.

\\\\\\\\\\\\\\\\\\\\\\\\\\\\\\\\\\\\\\\

Cat had been distant since Paul's ghost story.

Things did not improve once the eagle adventure was underway.

They rode single file for as long as the trail followed the river, and Cat complained about being stuck last, eating everyone else's dust. When the trail turned away from the water, Fletch led them through a jumbled section of rocky outcrops. Vertical walls rose above their heads, throwing them into shadows. The trail twisted and turned. At every fork, Fletch consulted a map that Mr. Bridle had marked up for them.

Rivka, who was riding second to last, turned around in the saddle to talk to Cat. "This is cool, isn't it? Like being in a maze." Cat glowered at her so ferociously that Rivka whipped back around in the saddle without another word.

An hour later, the rock maze spat them out onto a wide expanse of grass, and the horses fanned out. Fletch and Sam trotted ahead, making for the cliff with the eagle's nest. Even without binoculars, Rivka could see the giant pile of sticks on a narrow ledge. The rock below was stained white from their droppings.

Madison and the three girls spread out until they were all riding side by side.

"Hey, look!" Lauren said, pointing excitedly. A huge bird swooped over the edge of the cliff and soared over their heads.

Rivka craned her neck to watch it pass over. "I've never seen an eagle before."

"I wish my mom were here," said Lauren. "She'd love it."

"Is she a bird-watcher like Sam?" Rivka asked.

"Nope, but she loves all things science and nature. That's the best part of homeschooling."

The eagle circled higher and higher until it was only a dark speck in the sky.

"Don't you get tired of being with your mom all the time?" Rivka asked, wondering what it would be like to have her mom teaching her stuff.

"Not really," said Lauren. "She's a great teacher."

Cat made a disgusted sound. "'My mom's a great teacher,'" she mocked.

"Well, she is," Lauren said, bristling.

Cat rolled her eyes. "Lucky you."

Rivka shifted uneasily in her saddle.

"Come on, Cat," Madison urged. "Don't pick a fight."

"What I want to know," Cat went on in the same needling tone, "is why your super-sweet, perfect mother shipped you off here for smoking a few measly cigarettes."

"Cat—" Madison warned.

"Seriously," Cat blustered. "Who flies off the handle for something like that? Her mom must not be *that* great."

Rivka could see that Lauren was getting more

and more upset. So were the horses. Rowdy must have sensed her discomfort because he shifted nervously beneath her. Lauren's grip on the reins was getting tighter and tighter, and her horse was getting twitchy.

"She thought I was getting in with a bad crowd," Lauren protested.

"You're homeschooled. Where's the crowd?"

Lauren reined her horse to a stop. "If you have to know, I got the cigarettes from a girl at my fencing studio. And you know what?" She was yelling now. "She was a lot like you—trouble!"

Cat's face contorted and turned bright red, and she kicked her heels into Bucky's sides. When the horse jolted into a run, Lauren's horse startled and she dropped her reins. Madison made a grab for them but missed, and the horse bolted with Lauren clinging to its back.

"Stay here!" Madison yelled at Rivka as she urged Snow White to follow Lauren.

Cat wheeled around on Bucky and raced back the way they had come.

"Stop!" Rivka yelled after her, but Cat kept going.

Panic buzzed through Rivka. Fletch and Sam were out of sight. Madison had caught up with

Lauren, and both horses were slowing down together. But Cat was leaving all by herself.

*Buddy system. Buddy system. Buddy system.*

The words pounded along with her thudding pulse.

They were supposed to stick together.

## CHAPTER TWENTY-TWO

**R**ivka watched Cat disappear behind an outcrop of rocks.

Her stomach knotted into a hard ball, and she thought she might throw up. Going after Cat definitely meant getting in trouble—big trouble. But she had to do something. She couldn't leave Cat alone in the big wild everything. Especially not when she was upset. Ma Etty wanted them to look out for each other, and Rivka didn't want anything bad to happen to Cat. Especially not now that they were starting to be friends.

Rachel Jacobs, the pioneer woman with her own cattle brand, would have gone after Cat. No doubt about it. Rivka sat tall in the saddle, leaned forward, and gave a squeeze with her legs. The sturdy pony broke into a trot, and Rivka urged him on the trail after Cat.

It seemed like it took forever to get back to the place where the trail dove into the rocks, and when they did, it was darker inside the narrow passage than she remembered. She called to Cat and got nothing back but her own voice, echoing in the shadows.

Rowdy paused, sensing her hesitation, and swung his head from side to side like there was something making him nervous too. She thought of the ghost children in Paul's story and shuddered.

"It's okay," she murmured to Rowdy, trying to convince herself as well.

Together, they headed into the maze.

At the first fork in the trail, Rivka asked Rowdy to halt so she could figure out which was the right way to go. He shook his head, and the bridle jingled. Then he waited. Suddenly it was quiet. Her ears strained to hear some sound of Cat ahead of her.

Nothing.

Rivka tipped her head up to the slot of blue sky visible overhead. A whistling, keening sound filtered down into the shadowed silence.

"It's wind," she told herself. "Wind overhead."

But it rose and fell almost like voices, and she shivered.

"Cat!" she called again, and her voice reverberated off the walls of rock.

She looked again at the fork in the trail. The sand on the left-hand side was trampled. That must have been the way they'd come. She leaned forward, and Rowdy followed her body's cue. As they walked, she scanned for landmarks, anything that might tell her which way they'd come. Cat had to be heading for camp.

She wouldn't run away, would she?

Out here, there was nowhere to run. Rivka clung to the idea of the campfire and Paul. He'd be there, or he'd be back soon. He'd make everything okay.

The path twisted and turned. The walls were even higher overhead now. At the next fork, Rowdy was walking on solid rock, not sand. Nothing looked familiar. There were no hoof prints to follow. Rivka had no idea which one led back to camp.

Rivka stopped again to listen, trying not to think of ghosts and disaster. For a long moment, she waited, but the fear of being lost rose in great waves. Rivka was about to head down the right-hand trail when she felt Rowdy stiffen underneath her. His ears flicked forward and back and in all directions.

All at once, she heard a tangle of sounds, tumbling against the rock walls. A guttural snarl from some large animal very nearby. The terrified scream of a horse. The pounding of hooves.

And then a high-pitched shriek and the thud of a body on the ground.

Rowdy snorted and stomped, shifting nervously from hoof to hoof.

Rivka tried to calm him, stroking his neck and murmuring to him. *Easy, boy. Easy, boy.* Her own breath was coming a mile a minute. She had to see what had happened. She had to find Cat!

The urge to hurry raced through her.

"Come on," she said to Rowdy, clucking her tongue at him, but no matter how hard she dug her heels into his sides, the pony wouldn't move.

Rivka slid off his back and slipped the reins over Rowdy's head.

The rock walls pressed against her.

The wind voices twisted overhead.

*Hurry, hurry, hurry.*

She was small, so small, nothing but a speck of dust.

Rivka clutched the reins, one hand near Rowdy's chin and the other near the knot in the leather.

She had to keep going.

# CHAPTER TWENTY-THREE

**W**hat Rivka saw around the next bend made her heart batter her ribcage.

Cat was sprawled in the middle of the trail.

Terror dug claws into Rivka.

Was she . . . ?

Rivka couldn't think it. She pulled the pony toward Cat.

Suddenly Cat's body convulsed. Her mouth opened and closed, sucking air, trying to fill her stunned lungs. One of her arms twitched and fell back against the dirt.

Rivka fought the urge to turn and run.

Cat's eyes widened when she saw Rivka, and her ragged gasps of breath sped up.

"It's okay," Rivka murmured even though she was pretty sure this was about as far from okay as you could get. Cat's pupils seemed too large, and she moaned when she tried to sit up. Rivka put a hand on her shoulder and eased her down. "Don't move yet. Let's figure out where you're hurt."

"Everywhere," Cat groaned. "Everything hurts."

Scattered bits of first aid from the babysitter class she'd taken came to mind. *Don't move the victim if you suspect a spinal injury. Stanch bleeding. Watch for signs of shock.* It was a hodgepodge of words that seemed to mean next to nothing. Except the idea of wounds. Rivka ran her hands over Cat's shoulders and down her arms and legs. She wasn't bleeding anywhere. That was good.

"Can you wiggle your fingers?" she asked.

Cat wiggled.

"How about your feet?"

Cat's boots traced an arc as she swung them.

In the movies, an injured person got their eyes checked. Rivka bent over Cat's face, holding up her index finger. "Watch my finger," she said, moving it slowly from left to right and back again. Cat was tracking her, and her pupils were the same size. "You can see, right?" she asked.

Cat closed her eyes. "I can see."

She took several labored breaths, wincing when she tried to breathe too deeply.

"What's wrong?"

"Hurts."

Cat still didn't open her eyes, but her chest rose and fell more regularly.

"Cat?"

She opened her eyes and locked them with Rivka's.

"Do you want to try to sit up?" Rivka asked. The girl nodded.

Rivka slid her arm under Cat's shoulders, helped her into a sitting position, and unclipped her riding helmet.

Cat wrapped her arms around herself, leaning heavily against Rivka. "My ribs hurt."

"Do you think they're broken?"

Cat tried to shrug but gasped at the pain. "Don't know. Could be."

Inch by inch, pausing often so Cat could catch her breath, Rivka helped her move out of the center of the trail and find a rock to lean against. "Let's rest a little and then figure out what we need to do," she said, retrieving water and granola bars from Rowdy's saddlebags.

Cat nodded and took the water bottle.

After a moment, Rivka asked, "What happened?"

Cat shook her head slowly, looking down at her hands like they held some answer she couldn't quite grasp. "I'm not sure. Everything happened so fast. Something scared Bucky. I hit the ground before I even knew what was happening."

Rivka glanced around the high-walled slot of rock they were in. The sun was nearly overhead now, and it pounded down on them. A few scraggly plants clung to life in the cracks, but other than that it was stark and empty. "What do you think it was?" she asked, remembering the snarl.

"Ghost," Cat said, grimacing at the joke no one in their right mind would think was funny.

Rivka's face tightened. "Could it have been a wolf?"

"Paul said there weren't any," Cat wailed.

"What about Bucky?" Rivka asked.

"He took off that way." Cat pointed down the trail. "We'll never catch him. What if he's lost?"

Rivka bit her lower lip. "Aren't they supposed to be able to find their own way home?"

"What about us? What are we going to do?"

Rivka took stock: two girls and one pony in

the middle of nowhere. "We're going to do what Rachel Jacobs would have done," she said. "We're getting out of this mess. We'll try to follow Bucky. Can you ride?"

Cat took a deep breath. "Let's see."

Rivka stood, dusted the sand off her pants, and held out her hands. Cat took them, and Rivka could feel her shaking. "Ready?"

Cat nodded.

"On three," said Rivka, and at the end of the countdown, she pulled Cat to her feet as gently as she could.

"Oh, man," said Cat, panting hard, but she stayed upright, looping her arm around Rivka's shoulder.

Getting her on Rowdy's back was harder. Cat nearly fainted from the pain in her ribs, but the patient little pony stood still while Rivka helped her into the saddle. Once Cat was up, Rivka led the pony, and they set off in the direction Cat's horse had fled.

Cat didn't complain again, but Rivka could tell that every step hurt. After about twenty minutes, they reached another fork in the trail and paused, peering down one path and then the other.

"Does this look familiar to you?" Rivka asked.

"Not at all."

"Me either."

The weather was shifting. It was still hot, but clouds were gathering. Huge thunderheads billowed in the sky above, white and fluffy like sheep on top but dark and heavy with rain on the bottoms.

The wind picked up.

Rivka could hear it whistling overhead, and gusts of hot air billowed through the narrow canyon where they walked. Any trace of their passing had been scoured away by the wind.

"Right or left?" asked Cat.

Rivka looked from one path to the other. Nothing differentiated them. Rock, sand, and lime-green lichen in both directions. "Let's take the wider path," she suggested, and they did. After another half an hour, the temperature dropped suddenly. The air around them felt charged. Thunder rumbled in the distance. Somewhere not too far away, it was raining.

"I need to rest," said Cat, and Rivka nodded. Her feet ached in her cowboy boots.

"Let's go a little farther. Try to find some protection. I think it's going to rain on us."

Around the next bend, the trail widened. The

walls around them were less vertical and more like great jumbled piles of rock. It made Rivka think they might be close to a way out of the confusing twists and turns. A few scraggly pines grew out of the barest patches of soil. Behind them was a rock overhang that looked promising. There were also a few tufts of grass for Rowdy.

After Cat was as comfortable as she could be, Rivka decided to unsaddle Rowdy and replace his bridle with the halter and rope that were in her saddlebag. As soon as she did, he smacked his lips and went for the grass. "Silly old pig," she said, scratching him under the forelock. "You must be tired too." She tied Rowdy to one of the trees within reach of the grass and put his tack on a rocky ledge.

When she plopped down next to Cat, she groaned. "I'm so tired."

Rivka checked her watch. Almost four o'clock. Surely, Madison and Fletch and Paul were looking for them. Surely, they would find them soon. But find them where? She had no doubt that they had taken a wrong turn. This bowl-shaped area of rock and sand was unmistakable. They had not come this way.

How would Paul and the trainers know where to look?

Like her fragmented knowledge of first aid, another scrap of information, learned maybe during the one and only year Rivka was a Girl Scout, rose from the depths of her brain. *If you're lost, stay put.* They hadn't stayed put. Probably they'd made their situation a whole lot worse.

They were in trouble.

Big trouble.

Broken ribs.

A lost horse.

Two girls alone in the middle of nowhere.

Rivka had no idea how they were going to get home.

## CHAPTER TWENTY-FOUR

The sky darkened.

Wind whipped across the rock face where they huddled.

Rivka squinted her eyes against the flying dust that needled her face.

Cat leaned into Rivka. "What if they don't find us?" she asked in a small voice.

Rivka tucked her arm around Cat. "Paul won't leave us out here."

"My mom probably wouldn't even notice."

The words made Rivka's chest tighten. It was Friday night. Back at home, the table was set. Her mother was lighting Shabbat candles. Her father was holding up the glass of grape juice. There was a warm loaf of braided challah bread.

She wanted so badly to be at that table.

Lightning crackled in the distance, and the air smelled like rain.

"I'm so sorry I got us into this," Cat blurted. "Lauren was driving me crazy with her perfect mom and her perfect dad and her perfect homeschool." Cat looked like she was going to cry again. "And then she called me *trouble*. My stepdad says that."

"Ouch," said Rivka.

"I hear it all the time. *Cat the troublemaker. Cat the screwup.*"

"She didn't mean that."

A muscle in Cat's cheek twitched and she bit her lip. "She said it."

A tremendous crack of lightning split the sky and the thunder boomed right overhead, startling both girls and the pony. Rowdy stomped and huffed and pulled against his rope.

"Thanks for coming after me," said Cat.

Rivka leaned close enough for a shoulder bump. "Buddy system. Ma Etty's orders."

"I shouldn't have taken off."

"Probably not."

The rain began. Fat droplets hit the ground.

Rivka urged Rowdy to come closer so they could use his body as a windbreak.

"Will you tell me what happened with the car?" Rivka asked.

Cat sighed. "I overheard my mom and stepdad planning a vacation. They were gonna take my little brothers and my little sister—they're his kids and I'm not—and leave me with the neighbor. I guess I wandered a little farther than usual."

Somehow it comforted Rivka to imagine Cat behind the wheel, music loud, the open road, her hair flying. "Did you get very far?"

Cat shook her head. "Not far enough."

Another bolt of lightning sliced the dark clouds.

An avalanche of thunder rumbled over them, bringing the heaviest rain Rivka had ever seen. The girls held Rowdy's saddle blanket over their heads, but icy rivulets slid down their arms and necks and backs. Within seconds, they were soaked. A small river formed in the center of the trail, bulging and rushing. Rivka kept her eyes glued on the twisting water, hoping it wouldn't get any bigger and obliterate dry land completely. She didn't think they could climb up and out of the rocks, not with Cat's injury, and Rowdy would never be able to do it.

She considered untying him and letting him find his own way out, but thinking of being without his sturdy presence made her want to cry.

Cat trembled next to her. "I'm scared. I've never been so scared in my entire life."

"I have," said Rivka in a whisper.

The girls clung to each other, and as the storm pummeled them, Rivka told Cat about her cousins and Passover and the synagogue and how a few lines of red paint can mean *I hate you* and *I wish you were dead*.

# CHAPTER TWENTY-FIVE

**A**fter that, all they could do was wait.

Wait for the storm to stop.

Wait for the sun to dry them.

Wait for someone to come.

By the time it was over, the girls were cold and wet and exhausted. It seemed to them that the whole world—past, present, and future—was nothing but blasting wind and driving rain and angry gray.

But eventually the clouds cleared and the air warmed. Judging from the angle of the sun and the rumbling of her stomach, Rivka guessed it was dinnertime. The girls took off their soaked shirts, wrung them out, and put them back on again.

"Are there any more snacks in the saddlebags?" Cat

asked. Rivka rummaged through them and came up with a bag of jerky, which they split. "What are we going to do?" Cat said, handing Rivka the last piece.

"I don't know," she sighed, noticing how quickly the sun was dropping toward the horizon. Staying put was starting to seem like a terrible idea. Exhausted as she was, the thought of spending the night out here without a flashlight or sleeping bag made her skin crawl. "I think we should keep going. Try to find our way out of here."

"And end up where?"

Rivka shrugged. After all the twists and turns of the trail through the rock maze, she wasn't sure where they were. "If we can get out of these rocks and find the river, we can find our way back to camp."

Cat looked dubious.

"Got a better idea?"

"No," Cat admitted.

"You should ride," Rivka told Cat, and she began saddling Rowdy. The pony poked her with his nose and snuffled.

Rivka led Rowdy as he carried Cat.

They walked until the dusk deepened, turning the sky the color of a bruise in the east and of smoke in the west.

Right foot, left foot, right, left—Rivka watched the toes of her boots as she scuffed along. She was beyond tired, beyond hungry, and beyond scared. She moved in a numb sort of floating. The connection between her brain and her limbs had gone patchy. If she thought too hard about walking, her legs tangled. If she lost what little focus she clung to, she practically fell asleep on her feet.

They reached a fork in the trail. Without pausing, Rivka led Rowdy toward the wider path. Without landmarks and without a map, it was the only choice that made sense. Several times they'd reached dead ends and had to backtrack. Those steps, the repeats, were the hardest.

Two steps down the wider path, the halter rope in Rivka's hand went taut, pulling her to a stop, and she nearly fell.

"Come on, boy," she said, giving the rope a tug.

He pulled against her, dragging her back.

"What's going on?" said Cat, jolting awake at the sudden change of direction. She clung to the pommel, trying to make sense of what was happening.

Rivka found her balance and slid her hand up the halter rope until her fist gripped the rope near Rowdy's chin. His head was lifted and his eats swiveled in all directions. In another circumstance, it might have been funny. She might have made a joke about how he was part rabbit, but right now, it made the hair on the back of her neck stand up. She felt like something was watching them.

The light was nearly gone, the world dissolving from color into black and gray. She did not like how the darkness hid the details around her. Rowdy took two more steps backward, pulling the rope through her hand, and stood with his front legs splayed.

"It's okay, Rowdy," she said, trying to keep the trembling out of her voice. But even as inexperienced as she was, Rivka knew that he was nervous about something. "I think," she said to Cat, as low and steady as she could, "that you need to hold on. He might run."

"I can't fall again," said Cat. "I'm scared."

Rowdy sensed her agitation and tensed. She remembered what Madison said about Rowdy needing all the right cues from her. "You've got to stay calm," she told Cat. "We're going to try this again."

Rivka led Rowdy away from the fork in the trail and back the way they'd come until they reached a place where she could make a wide circle and return to where they'd started.

But when she tried again to lead him down the fork, he balked a second time.

"What's bugging you, Rowdy?" she murmured, stroking his neck. "We've got to try and get home."

Suddenly, Rowdy stretched out his muzzle, lifting his upper lip and sucking air in and out, in and out, like a person hyperventilating. Once again, Rivka had the sensation of being watched. She peered into the growing darkness, trying to make out shapes from shadows.

Cat let out her breath in a long, low hiss. "There's something down there."

Movement.

A shadow slipping through darker shadows, sinuous as a snake but far larger.

The shape paused in the center of the trail twenty feet from the girls. Long legs, muscled back, velvety coat. Its enormous, broad head swung toward them, round eyes flaring in the dim light. Its tail flicked.

Rivka froze. She was eye to eye with a giant cat. *Mountain lion. Cougar. Puma.*

All the names she'd ever heard for this animal tumbled through her head. None of them came close to capturing the creature. Powerful, beautiful, terrifying. She held her breath and prayed, not in words or even thoughts but in the frantic surging of her blood. Electricity coursed through her skin. For a split second, neither girl nor beast moved.

The mountain lion snarled, a gravelly, thunderous rumble. Rivka felt it in her chest like a punch. Cat gasped, and Rivka knew she recognized the sound. This was the animal that had spooked Bucky. It lowered its huge head, stretching toward them, low and lithe. The cougar's eyes were locked on Rivka. It extended a paw, took a step toward them.

And another.

The rabbi's words filled Rivka.

*I am but dust and ashes.*

*The world was created for me.*

And in that instant, both of those things were equally true.

Behind Rivka, Cat's breath came in short, staccato bursts. The pony pawed the ground.

The mountain lion was a coiled spring.

A single thought penetrated Rivka's panic. It was as if Rachel Jacobs spoke from the grave—*STAND UP!*

Rivka dropped Rowdy's reins, threw her hands high above her head, and yelled as loud as she could.

The guttural cry echoed off the rock walls, reverberating through the rock maze.

For a second, the mountain lion held her gaze and Rivka's heart froze in her chest, and then, without warning, it leapt up the jumbled rocks and disappeared into the night.

## CHAPTER TWENTY-SIX

For a long minute, neither girl moved or spoke. The air around them settled in a blanket of quiet.

Cat slid off of Rowdy's back, wincing, and went to Rivka's side. "Is it gone?"

Rivka's head ached from peering into the blackness for a flicker of a tail or the glow of gigantic eyes. The pony huffed and nosed his muzzle into Rivka's shoulder. She leaned into Rowdy.

"He's not scared anymore," she said to Cat. "So I don't think we need to be." She scratched Rowdy in his favorite spot. "You're so good," she breathed, running her hand down the pony's neck. "Such a good horse."

"I want to get out of these rocks," said Cat.

"Me too," said Rivka. "Can you walk a bit?"

Cat nodded. Together they shuffled along the trail, feeling with their feet for rocks that could trip them. Rowdy seemed happy enough to follow. After about ten minutes a half moon rose, turning everything silver and making it easier to walk. When the trail emerged from the rock fall, they could see for a long way in all directions.

The hillside sloped gently down to the river, which shone silver in the moonlight. They scanned up and down the river looking for landmarks, something familiar that would show them the way back to camp. The adrenaline from their encounter with the mountain lion had drained away, and Rivka's exhaustion had returned. They'd have to stop soon.

"If we're going to have to spend the night, I think we should try to get to the river."

Cat took a deep breath. "Makes sense. Rowdy needs water."

"So do we. The bottle's empty."

"I'm so tired."

Rivka could hear an edge of pain behind her words. "Do you want to ride the rest of the way?"

"Is that okay?" asked Cat in a small voice. "It's your turn."

Rivka squeezed her hand. "I'm okay."

She helped Cat mount, feeling a deep ache in every muscle. She picked her way along a game trail that led down the slope toward the water. Her legs were robot limbs. Eventually the sharp stab of blisters in her cowboy boots punctuated every step. She'd pay a thousand dollars for sneakers right now, and a helicopter rescue and dry underwear and . . .

"Did you see that?" Cat asked.

Rivka felt a jolt of fear. "What? Where? Is it the mountain lion?"

Cat pointed toward the river, and Rivka thought she saw a flicker of light.

There it was again.

A yellow twinkle in the thick brush along the river.

"Hello?" Rivka yelled. "Is anyone down there?"

The light paused, pointed toward them. "Rivka? Cat?" The man's voice was faint, but they both knew exactly who it was.

"Paul!" the girls yelled together. "It's us!"

He let out a triumphant whoop, and the girls saw the light bob toward them, a beacon leading them home.

Madison wrapped Cat's ribs with an Ace bandage.

Paul made cocoa, warm and extra-chocolatey.

Fletch built up the fire, and Lauren wrapped a sleeping bag around Rivka's shoulders. Sam took care of Rowdy. Everyone was talking a mile a minute.

"Cat, Bucky came back hours ago."

"We were so worried."

"I'm so sorry."

"What happened?"

The words blurred in a collage of sound. All Rivka wanted to do was stare into the flames and eat dinner and bask in the warmth of being with the others. It felt like she'd been gone a lifetime. When Cat told the story of what had happened to them, she made Rivka sound like some kind of hero.

After they had explained everything, Rivka snuggled down into the slick fabric of the sleeping bag and curled into a ball, finally warm. But, tired as she was, she couldn't fall asleep right away. While they were lost, Rivka had been scared and tired and worried. She'd felt very small and insignificant, but now something bloomed in the middle of her chest—a warm surge of pride in what she had done.

Rivka fell asleep satisfied that she'd done all right in the big wild everything.

\\\\\\\\\\\\\\\\\\\\\\\\\\\\\\\\\\\\\\\\\\\\

They rode back to the ranch the next day. On the trail, Rivka kept leaning down to stroke Rowdy's neck with her free hand. "You know," she told him, "you're awfully sweet for a stubborn old pony."

He snorted at her as if he knew exactly what she was saying, and promptly reached for the nearest clump of grass.

When the trail was wide enough, she and Cat rode side by side. Bucky's jostling gait was painful for Cat, and Rivka's own muscles were tight and sore.

"Hot bath," she said, when they caught the first glimpse of the ranch house.

Cat sighed. "That would be fantastic."

"You can go first."

Cat smiled at her. "Nah. It's all you, fearless leader."

Rivka grinned back.

As it turned out, Rivka did indeed get the

first soak. Etty bustled and clucked over them like a mother hen before hustling Cat into the truck for a trip to urgent care for an X-ray. As Rivka's fingers and toes turned wrinkly in the bath, she wondered if she and Cat were going to have consequences for running off like they did. She thought they probably deserved it but really hoped Ma Etty wouldn't assign shoveling manure or moving firewood. Her poor muscles screamed from the exertion of the previous day. She wasn't sure she could walk back to the bunkhouse, much less do any more physical labor.

She was half asleep on the couch when Ma Etty and Cat came home.

"Nothing's broken," Cat announced.

"She's got some amazing bruises though," Ma Etty added. "I'm talking eggplants."

"Can I see?" Lauren asked, and Cat lifted the back of her shirt to show the mottled purple markings on her ribcage.

"That's impressive," said Madison. "You're going to have to take it easy for a few days."

"What about riding?" Cat asked. "We don't have much time left in the summer."

Mr. Bridle chuckled and slid an arm around Ma

Etty's waist. "You've done it again, Henrietta. Taken another perfectly normal girl and made her wild about horses."

Ma Etty gave him a playful nudge. "That's called character-building. And I'm excellent at it!"

# CHAPTER TWENTY-SEVEN

The next day, Ma Etty intercepted Rivka and Cat after breakfast. Once the other kids had left with Madison and Fletch, she and Mr. Bridle sat them down at the big table for a serious talk.

"Your parents are coming to get you early," Ma Etty explained.

The girls exploded. "What? No!"

"You can't make us go home," Rivka protested. "I had to go after her. You said buddy system!"

"It wasn't her fault," Cat burst out. "I'm the one who ran off. Rivka shouldn't get in trouble at all!"

Mr. Bridle calmed them like spooked horses. "Easy there. Settle down."

Rivka and Cat spluttered into silence.

"Your parents are coming because they need to see for themselves that you're okay," Ma Etty explained. "They were pretty upset when I called to tell them what had happened."

"Why can't we just talk to them on the phone?" said Rivka.

"Yeah," said Cat. "It's not like my mom wants to come anyway."

Ma Etty gazed at her. "Your mom was really worried, Cat. She's going to call in about an hour to talk to you."

"Don't hold your breath," Cat sighed. "She'll probably forget."

Ma Etty patted her hand. "It's never too late to find your way back together, especially if you stick around to make it happen."

Before Cat could argue, Mr. Bridle said, "We still need to talk about what happened out there." Rivka squeezed her hands in her lap, bracing for a lecture. "You made some choices—dangerous choices—that put you in harm's way and put a huge burden on Paul, Madison, and Fletch. Henrietta and I are mighty glad that you are home safe, but it is still our obligation to address your actions."

Rivka chewed the inside of her cheek. Letting

down the Bridles made her feel minuscule.

"Normally," the old man continued, "we think that good, old-fashioned manual labor helps kids get their heads back on their necks."

"But we know," said Ma Etty, "that you are both feeling a little ragged from your adventure." She said that last word carefully, like she wasn't making the case that it was a good thing or a bad thing, just that it was a thing that happened. Rivka felt a tiny surge of hopefulness. Maybe their punishment wouldn't be too terrible.

"We are going to ask you to spend the afternoon helping make signs for the anti-immigrant rally tomorrow," said Mr. Bridle.

Rivka felt the knot in her stomach start to form again.

"We are part of the counter-protest," Ma Etty explained. "We have to stand with Álvaro and Elias and the rest of our friends here."

"Show us what to do," said Rivka, feeling tired to her core. It was more than physical exhaustion. She felt overwhelmed by how much meanness there could be in the world.

Cat spread newspapers down on the front porch.

Rivka opened the jars of paint and brought out a jar of water for rinsing the brushes.

"Here's the poster board," said Ma Etty, handing over a stack of white sheets.

Mr. Bridle put down an armload of thin wooden boards, each about two feet long and two inches thick, and handed Rivka a roll of duct tape. "Wrap a bit of this around the end of each stick before you put on the signs. I don't want anyone to get splinters. I'll be right back with the staple gun."

When the porch door shut behind him, Cat leaned against the porch railing and looked out at the arena where Lauren and Sam were learning to ride their horses around a set of three barrels. "Lucky ducks."

Rivka agreed. If her parents insisted on taking her early, she'd hardly get any more time with Rowdy, and back at home, she wouldn't have him at all. That was too awful for words.

Mr. Bridle returned and handed her the staple gun. "Don't worry," he said. "I'll make sure you get to ride tomorrow. Rowdy misses you."

Rivka gazed up at him. "Does he really?"

Mr. Bridle grinned and pointed to the pasture

on the far side of the house. A brown nose poked between the slats of the fence, pointing in her direction. "Now get to work," said the old man. "Time's a-wasting." She picked up a piece of poster board. "Oh, and by the way," said Mr. Bridle, sticking his head back out the porch door, "Paul thought you might be interested in this." He held out a book.

"What's that?" Cat asked.

"*Jewish Pioneers of the Old West*," said Rivka, reading the title as she took it from Mr. Bridle. She flipped through the pages. It fell open to a page full of cattle brands. Sure enough, there was the squished-together R and J of Rachel Jacobs, right next to the brands of her sisters Hannah and Bella. She flipped to the index and looked up Rachel Jacobs. On page sixty-seven was a grainy old photograph of the cabin on the river. A curly-haired woman about her mom's age stood by the door with a rifle over one shoulder. The caption read *Cattle woman Rachel Jacobs was a crack shot.*

"Wow," she said, holding the book out so Cat could see the picture. "That's Rachel Jacobs."

"No one is going to mess with her."

Ma Etty rounded the corner of the house, followed by seven chickens. "Nobody should mess with me either," she called. "Paint now. Read later. Everyone is coming over after dinner to get their signs." With that, she snapped her fingers at one of the chickens, saying, "Come on, Broccoli, let's get you back to the coop."

"I wonder if there is one named Cabbage," Cat said in a not-so-quiet whisper.

"Not yet," Ma Etty called, "but that's a good name for a chicken!"

The girls collapsed into giggles.

When they finally collected themselves, Rivka put a fresh piece of poster board on top of the newspapers and picked up one of the stencils Ma Etty had left. *All Ranch Families Are Our Families.* Carefully, she centered it on the poster board and painted over the letters with dark green tempera paint. Rivka made five more before switching to the next message.

"Are you going to protest at the rally?" Cat asked, painting *No Hands, No Harvest* in red.

Rivka squinted at her poster board, trying to decide if she had the stencil level. The words leapt out at her: *Strong Together.* She believed that—she really did. Look at what had just happened to her and Cat. They had stuck together and made it back in one piece. But going to the rally? That was an entirely different kind of challenge.

"I don't know," she said, finally. "I mean, I want to help Álvaro, but . . ."

". . . it's still scary?" Cat offered.

"Yeah," Rivka agreed, lifting the stencil with her fingertips. "Maybe I'll work up to it."

They painted until the porch was covered with signs neatly lined up to dry.

"You know that story you told me during the storm, the one about your synagogue?" Cat asked, swirling her paintbrush in the jar of water.

"What about it?" said Rivka, chewing on her lower lip.

"Is that why you don't want to do your bat mitzvah?"

Rivka shrugged.

"Because I think," Cat continued in a rush, "that if you can stand up to a mountain lion that's about to eat you, you could go back to your synagogue."

"Why do you care?" she asked, unable to meet Cat's eyes.

Her friend snorted. "I hear the after-party is killer."

Rivka rolled her eyes and considered the bat mitzvah. It would be a lot of work to get ready. She'd have to learn a bunch of prayers and how to chant from the Torah. She'd have to write a speech and do a community service project. It all felt over-whelming. Rivka snuck a glance at Cat. "Would you come?"

"Sure."

"All the way from Ohio?"

Cat raised one eyebrow. "Is there a chicken named Broccoli?"

On cue, the little flock of chickens came wad-dling around the corner, pecking and gabbling.

Maybe she could do it. Maybe it was like getting un-lost, a matter of taking it one step at a time.

Sam and Lauren rounded the corner after the chickens.

"Are you slackers almost done?" Sam yelled.

Lauren gestured to them. "Time for Frattleprat."

Rivka looked at the poster board nearest to her. It said *All Hands Build America.* That meant Álvaro, and Mr. Bridle's Paiute ancestors, and her. If Rachel Jacobs could run a ranch all by herself in the middle of Colorado, it seemed to Rivka that she could stand up and say *I'm Jewish.* Her family would be there, and her Jewish community, and maybe even Cat.

"We're coming," Cat said, washing the last of the paintbrushes. "Wait for us."

And she and Rivka joined the others.

# CHAPTER TWENTY-EIGHT

**M**r. Bridle did not let Rivka down. The next day, she was back in the saddle. Cat watched from the porch, nursing her sore ribs, as Rivka and Rowdy cantered around the arena. The sturdy little pony did everything she asked, and Rivka let the joy sink into her bones. This feeling, this connection—she wanted to put it in her pocket with the slip of paper about the world being created for her.

When she reined in at the end of the lesson, flushed and sweaty, Mr. Bridle said, "I like what I see, Rivka. You've become such a strong rider."

She grinned at him. "Rowdy is a great horse!"

"You make a good team."

She dawdled as she untacked Rowdy and brushed him down. Leaving Quartz Creek Ranch early was the last thing she wanted to do. When she turned the pony out in the pasture with Bucky and the rest of the horses, she wished she could stay the rest of the summer.

\\\\\\\\\\\\\\\\\\\\\\\\\\\\\\\\\\\\\\\

After chore time, Sam and Lauren decided to go birdwatching.

"You two should come," said Lauren.

Sam held up his binoculars. "We're looking for the belted kingfisher burrows that Fletch told us about."

"I wish," Rivka replied.

"Our parents are coming," said Cat, looking none too pleased.

Lauren frowned. "Do you guys really have to leave early?"

Rivka slumped on the porch. "Apparently."

"That sucks," said Sam. "Come on, Lauren."

Cat scowled at him. "Love you too, Big Boy."

Lauren scurried onto the porch to hug the girls. "We'll be back before you go. Don't leave without saying good-bye." Then she turned to catch up with Sam.

Rivka and Cat watched them go and then waited on the porch together, silent and nervous.

Cat's mom arrived first, calling out to her daughter as soon as she got out of the car. She was a small woman with lines around her eyes and a slump to her shoulders. She took a few tentative steps toward Cat and paused in front of the porch steps, waiting for some sign. Rivka wondered if Cat could do it—if she could reach out, instead of running away.

Mother and daughter stared at each other for a long moment. Finally, Cat's mom said, "Are you okay?"

Cat made a sour face. "Do you care?"

"Oh, Cat, how can you ask that?"

"You never have time for me. Why should now be any different?"

Cat's mom looked as if she might cry. "I never, ever meant for you to feel ignored. You know that, right?"

Cat didn't say anything.

"When I heard what happened on your pack trip, I was so scared," said her mom. "I don't want to lose you."

Rivka felt Cat hesitate and heard the hitch in her breath.

"I don't want to be lost," said Cat in a small voice.

Rivka could feel the sadness in her friend. She held her breath, hoping.

"Family is complicated," said Cat's mom, looking like she was about to cry. "Especially ours, and I know I haven't been there for you the way I should have been. That's going to change."

"Really?"

Her mom gave a tentative smile. "I promise."

Cat chewed on her lower lip. Mother and daughter watched each other. Finally, Cat said, "What I want is more time with you, just the two of us. Okay? That hasn't happened in a long time."

Her mom's face lit up. "Oh, sweetie, I want that too!" She held out her arms, and Cat took the porch steps quickly. They embraced, and from the porch, Rivka watched her friend melt into her mother's arms.

"I want you to show me everything on the ranch," Cat's mom said, and the two of them headed toward the barn.

Ten minutes later, another rental car rumbled down Bridlemile Road.

Rivka twisted the hem of her T-shirt into a knot. Suddenly, she didn't feel ready for this. Not by a long shot

Her little brother Eli was the first one out of the car. He threw the door open and bounded up the porch steps, diving into her arms. "Hey, Little Little," she said, ruffling his hair and using his old nickname. Over the top of his head, she watched her parents and Noah get out of the car and stretch.

They had all come—the whole family, even Noah, who had to leave B'nai B'rith camp early. Her mom smelled like warm challah, and her dad's beard scuffed her cheek, just like always. Rivka couldn't speak. Not yet. Even though there was so much to say.

Eli tugged on her arm. "I want to meet the hero pony."

Rivka took his hand. They found Rowdy in the back pasture. As soon as he saw her, the pony trotted up, nosing her pockets for treats. She showed Eli how to offer one on a flattened palm.

"His lips tickle," Eli said, grinning at her. "And his nose is so soft."

Her dad gave Rowdy a scratch.

Her mom put her hands on Rivka's shoulders and gave her a squeeze. "You've had quite a summer."

"Was there really a mountain lion?" Noah asked.

Rivka made a face like she could hardly believe it herself. "Yeah, there was. Cat and I were trying to find our way back to camp, and all of a sudden, Rowdy wouldn't let us keep going. He knew it was there, and he knew it wasn't safe. So Rowdy got stubborn, and he saved us."

"That sounds a little bit like a certain girl I know," said her dad.

Rivka frowned at him. "You mean the stubborn part?"

He nodded.

Rivka looked down at her feet. "Yeah. Sometimes . . . I think sometimes I'm stubborn when I get scared."

"Scared?" her dad said. "Of what, honey?" Rivka's throat tightened. Rowdy nudged her through the fence. She scratched under his forelock and looked out across the pasture. This moment felt as difficult as any she had faced all summer. "When I saw the synagogue at Passover, I didn't want to be Jewish anymore. I didn't want to think about what might happen."

As she spoke, her mother's eyes filled with tears. Her dad let out a long breath. "Oh, honey. We had no idea."

"I wish you had said something," said her mother in a choked voice. "We could have talked about it."

"I didn't know how to say it. I guess I . . . thought

it was obvious. But then you acted like nothing had changed and everything was fine, and I just got angry."

Her dad took Rivka's hands and gazed into her eyes. "We are so sorry that we didn't make you feel safe. That's on us. We let you down."

Rivka thought about that. "You know," she said slowly, "I don't think it's possible to feel safe all the time. But you can't let that stop you." And she wrapped her arms around her parents and hugged them tight.

And she wrapped her arms around her parents and hugged them tight. They stood that way for a while without speaking. Finally, her mom smiled gently and asked, "Are you ready to go home?"

"Well . . ." Rivka hesitated. "There's this rally in town later today, to support our immigrant friends. The Bridles and Cat and some other people are going. I was hoping you would take me before we drive back to Denver."

"That sounds important," her dad said.

Rivka gave Rowdy another treat. "I'm nervous," she told her parents. "But I really need to be there."

Mr. Bridle joined them at the pasture fence.

"It looks like we'll be staying a little longer," her dad told him.

"I'm glad," said Mr. Bridle.

"So I have this other idea . . ." Rivka began, wanting to catch Mr. Bridle while she could. "I will need to do a community service project if I'm going to have my bat mitzvah."

Her parents exchanged a smile. Mr. Bridle nodded. "Go on."

"And I was thinking that I could catalogue the homesteads of the Jewish pioneers in this area. I'll spend the winter doing research and come back here next summer to take pictures of all the sites."

"Some of them are pretty far away," he mused.

Rivka had thought of that too. "No problem. We'll ride."

He touched the brim of his cowboy hat. "We?"

"I'm coming!" Cat said, leading her mom toward them.

Rivka beamed at her. To Mr. Bridle she said, "Paul told me that you're really into the history of this area. Maybe you'd want to come with us."

The old man gazed at her. "I'll have to check in with Ma Etty."

"Think about it," Rivka pleaded. At that moment Ma Etty came out of the ranch house to invite them in for some pie. She was wearing a T-shirt that said

*If it involves a horse, I'm in.* A huge grin spread across Mr. Bridle's craggy face. "I guess you've got yourself a bat mitzvah project!"

\\\\\\\\\\\\\\\\\\\\\\\\\\\\\\\\\\\\\\\\\\\\\\

The last thing Rivka did before they left for the rally was say good-bye to Rowdy. She ran her fingers through his mane and leaned into his warm, strong neck.

"You have to keep an eye on Peanut. Teach him to be tough like you."

Rowdy huffed at her, and his breath smelled like sweet grass.

"I'll miss you," she said, through the lump in her throat, and the pony nuzzled her arm.

There was something extraordinary about Quartz Creek Ranch, about Ma Etty and Mr. Bridle, about Fletch and Madison, and especially about the horses.

They changed people.

*That's not quite right*, she thought.

Being on the ranch hadn't *changed* her, but it had given her time to figure some things out. As Rivka scratched under Rowdy's forelock and listened to the burbling creek, she knew these green pastures would always feel like home.

# ABOUT THE AUTHORS

**KIERSI BURKHART** grew up riding horses on the Colorado Front Range. At sixteen, she attended Lewis & Clark College in Portland and spent her young adult years in beautiful Oregon—until she discovered her sense of adventure was calling her elsewhere. Now she travels around with her best friend, a mutt named Baby, writing fiction for children of all ages.

**AMBER J. KEYSER** is happiest when she is in the wilderness with her family. Lucky for her, the rivers and forests of Central Oregon let her paddle, hike, ski, and ride horses right outside her front door. When she isn't adventuring, Amber writes fiction and nonfiction for young readers and goes running with her dog, Gilda.

# ACKNOWLEDGMENTS

We have loved our time on the ranch with the cowpokes (aka the team at Darby Creek), our ranch manager (aka agent Fiona Kenshole), our real-life horse trainer (aka Wendy Myers), and the best Jewish cowgirl ever (aka Ruth Feldman). It's hard to pack our saddlebags and go.

This book was inspired by the pack trips Amber went on as a child, one in Montana with a guide named Half-Way Earl and the other in the Mount Zirkel Wilderness in Colorado with her awesome Steamboat cousins. The pony in this book is loosely based on a sweet little Welsh pony named Peanut, who left her far too soon. Amber will always miss her mornings at the barn on Skyline.